SUCKERED

A RYLIE COOPER MYSTERY

STELLA BIXBY

FERRY TAIL PUBLISHING LLC

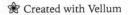

For my sweet Lily. Happy Birthday, beautiful! I love you!

R attlesnake wrangling was not on my bucket list.

When Brock radioed that he needed my assistance on the swim beach, I thought it would be for a found child, a fish hook injury, or even another dead body. I never imagined I'd end up face to face with a venomous monster.

The snake's stare mirrored my determination. I would not—could not—make a fool of myself.

The snake coiled its long brown and tan body, its head up, ready to strike. It shook its tail in the sand, the rattling sound muffled by gasps and whispers of the beachgoers with their smartphone cameras pointed at me.

I brandished my snake stick—a golf club with a hook welded onto the end—and tried to hook it under the belly of the beast like we'd practiced in training. I glanced back at the five-gallon snake bucket. The lid was off and ready to be quickly replaced trapping the snake safely inside.

How was I the only ranger at the reservoir right now who wasn't afraid of snakes? My heart thumped in my throat where the rope burns from my brush with death a couple of months ago had finally healed into small, angry red scars. Thankfully, the man responsible was no longer my supervisor, but that was another story.

The snake opened its mouth and hissed at the snake stick. I took a startled step backward, but instead of finding solid ground, my foot landed in what felt like a pile of quicksand.

The world slowed as my ankle twisted and I landed flat on my ass.

A high-pitched scream from behind me drew my attention away from the snake. The searing pain in my hand indicated what my diverted eyes didn't see—the snake sinking its fangs into my flesh.

A gasp stole through the crowd.

My mind blanked, and the world spun as the snake opened its mouth to attempt another bite.

Without thinking, I grabbed the snake with my left hand and threw it away from me—right at the feet of one of the trail rangers, Seamus.

"Bloody hell," Seamus said in his Irish brogue that practically made ladies beg him to write them tickets if only for the few extra minutes they'd have with him. "Yeh can't be throwin' snakes at people." He yanked the snake stick from my hand.

The snake coiled into position ready to strike, but it didn't faze Seamus. Like a pro, he hooked the stick under the snake's belly, deposited it into the bucket, and snapped the lid on top.

The crowd erupted in cheers, and Seamus shot them a cheeky grin.

"Don't worry about me." My vision blurred. "I'm only *dying* over here," I reminded them as panic flooded my chest.

I squeezed my eyes shut and grasped my wrist as hard as possible with my other hand trying to prevent the venom from spreading through my body. If I moved too much, I'd be dead in minutes. Bile crept up my throat.

"Yeh ain't dyin'," Seamus laughed, and the crowd roared along with him. "It's just a measly bullsnake. Not venomous."

I opened one eye and let it focus on the scruffy man looking down at me with one eyebrow raised. I released my wrist allowing blood flow back to my purpling hand and choked down the vomit.

"Hey lady," an angry-looking little girl walked over and stood right next to Seamus, her hands on her hips and her big blue eyes red from crying, "you sat on my sand castle."

So much for not making a fool of myself.

In a matter of minutes, I'd managed to discredit myself as a ranger, humiliate myself in front of a hundred park guests, get myself bitten by a *non*-venomous snake, *and* wreck a little girl's sand castle. There was no way I would get the full-time position.

"I—I'm sorry." I tried to stand, but my butt stayed cemented to the ground.

Brock, one of my fellow summer rangers or summies, as we're more affectionately known, offered a hand and yanked me to my feet.

"Thanks, Rylie. I would have helped, but I'm scared

shitless of snakes." An embarrassed blush hid Brock's usual testosterone-fueled façade. "At least I won't have to deal with them once I'm a cop."

Brock as a cop might have been scarier than being bitten by a rattlesnake, or bullshit snake, or whatever the hell it was called.

"Yeh both should have been able to handle it yourselves," Seamus said. "That's why we went through a week-long course on snake handling."

"I thought I could but . . ." I felt my cheeks blossoming into crimson circles. Thankfully the park guests had long forgotten about me and were returning to their weekend activities.

"Don't make the same mistake twice," Seamus said. He was only about five years older than my almost-thirty, but he acted like the wise old ranger wizard.

"Why are you even here?" I asked him. "Aren't you supposed to be patrolling the trails?"

He shrugged one broad shoulder. "I thought I'd come and check on yeh since the reservoir is so busy. And it's a good thing I did." He grabbed my hand in his examining the bloody puncture wounds. "We should probably get this cleaned up so it doesn't get infected."

Seamus poured hydrogen peroxide over the bite marks, and I did my best not to wince. Between the chemical smell and the physical sting, my eyes watered.

The shop office was basically a closet with a desk, a chair, and a first aid kit inside the shop where the trucks stayed when the park was closed. It wasn't the first time I'd been in there, but it was the first time I'd been in there with another person and it was pretty tight.

"Tricky little buggars, bullsnakes. Make themselves look like rattlers," he said as he wrapped my hand with gauze.

"How do you tell them apart then?" I asked. The air-conditioned shop was cool on one of the last warm days of fall.

"We went through all of this in training." He sighed.

We had gone through so much in training it made my head spin. I'd taken notes and even looked over them once I'd gotten home, but apparently it hadn't been enough.

"Bullsnakes don't have a rattle, so they keep their tails down. Rattlers hold their tails high and proud and shake those bastards like their lives depend on it." He ripped a strip of tape from the roll with his slightly crooked and coffee-stained teeth. "Rattlesnakes also have white borders around their spots and a triangular shaped head." A couple more pieces of tape and he was done. "Should heal in no time."

"Hey there," Shayla walked into the shop office where I examined my wrapped hand. "Everything okay?"

Seamus stepped away from me as if embarrassed. "No —yes—nothing happened."

"I think she can see that." I laughed. "Seamus wrapped my hand after a snake bit me."

"Oh my goodness, are you okay?" Shayla's blue eyes widened to the size of a Disney Princess'.

"It was just a bullsnake," Seamus said.

"I bet it still hurt." Shayla smiled.

"From the way she was complaining, yeh'd have thought it bit her arm off," Seamus said. "I should probably get back out to the trails. Yeh closin' up?" He asked Shayla.

"Yep, me and Antonio."

"Try to stay out of trouble." He winked, and her pale skin turned an innocent shade of pink. Antonio was a massive player and loved flirting with the summies, even though he was married, albeit unhappily.

"Antonio's harmless. Especially after what happened to Kyle. He just hasn't gotten his spunk back," Shayla said.

"His best friend was a murderous lunatic," Seamus said. "Served him right for what he got."

Anxiety welled in my chest. The mention of Kyle still brought back haunting memories of almost dying.

"Antonio will come around. He needs time," Shayla said. "But he only has eyes for one summie."

Both of their gazes turned to me. I smirked. "Whatever. Weren't you going to get back to the trails?"

"I'm going. I'm going."

Once Seamus had gone, Shayla looked at me. "Are you and Seamus—"

"No." I laughed. "No way. He winked at you, not me."

"He was just being Irish." She smiled. "Are we still going to work out or are you taking today off?"

We had been utilizing the untouched portion of the shop—the loft—to exercise. The full-timers didn't use it because the higher-ups had cameras to keep an eye on us, but Shayla and I didn't mind. Part of me even hoped they were watching so they knew how hard I was working out to be the best full-time ranger applicant.

"I'll just use my other hand," I said.

Shayla let out a breath. "Great. Thanks. You know I don't like to work out on my own."

"At least you'd have the place to yourself." I hopped off the table and followed her up the spiral metal staircase. The loft was brightly lit with a couch and TV, some nice new workout equipment, and lockers on one wall.

"I like the company." She stepped up onto the treadmill and started to walk. Her bright pink tank top showed off her farmers tan from working in the sun all summer in our signature short sleeve button down uniform shirts.

"I bet you'd like it more if it were Seamus . . ."

"Rylie!" She giggled.

"He was totally flirting with you," I poked.

"He'd never go for a girl like me."

"What do you mean a girl like you?" I yanked off my boots and uniform shirt and shoved them into the tiny locker that held my workout duffel bag.

"Slightly chunky." She looked down where her belly had been at the beginning of the summer.

"You're not chunky. You've lost how much now?"

"Almost thirty pounds," she said in a voice barely above a whisper. "But I don't want him to like me just because I've lost weight."

"I don't think your weight has any bearing on his affections. Your personality and heart are what make you beautiful."

"That's what everyone says about fat people."

I gasped. "You're not fat!" We both dissolved into laughter.

When we regained our composures, she asked, "Are

7

you going to work out or just stand there?"

I looked around before dropping my uniform cargo pants, shoving them into the locker and replacing them with a pair of black yoga pants.

From behind me, I heard a low whistle. I spun around to find none other than Antonio staring at my backside.

"You cannot help but disrobe in my presence." His Italian accent almost made me melt. The tight cotton t-shirt and expensive jeans covered with a pair of black leather chaps accentuated his rock-hard body. He held a helmet under one arm meaning he rode his Ducati to work.

"I had no idea you were there." I silently thanked the heavens it was laundry day, and the only underwear I had clean were full-coverage boy shorts rather than my usual thong. "What are you doing up here anyway?" I pointed up. "The cameras are still on."

Antonio lifted an eyebrow but didn't smile. "I am not the one changing in front of them."

He had a point.

"I am here to speak with Shayla about our upcoming shift."

I looked at the clock. "An hour early?"

He shrugged slightly. "It was a nice day for a ride."

"The Broncos game starts in five minutes. Don't you and your wife usually have a party for games?"

"The party was . . . canceled."

Perfect. He probably wanted to watch it on the loft's big screen. With us.

"Don't worry. You won't even know I'm here." He winked, and I silently chided my knees for going soft.

F irst and goal.

Broncos down by four.

My left fist hit its target. Hard.

Second and goal.

Fifteen seconds left in the game.

I swung my leg in a roundhouse kick. The impact of the bag sent shockwaves through my body.

Third and inches.

I paused. Held my breath.

Hudson threw, the ball spiraled, Navaro was there, arms outstretched—

"We interrupt this program to bring you breaking news." A red screen replaced the make or break moment in the game.

"What?" I shrieked at the screen.

"Oh come on!" Antonio yelled. After they'd done some patrolling, Antonio and Shayla returned to the loft to watch the last part of the game.

"Shhhh," Shayla waved her hand at our protests, "Listen."

"Prairie City High graduate and notorious drug trafficker Alex, Boy Boy, Johnson has escaped from an Arizona prison today and is believed to be in the area."

The newscaster showed a picture of a large man with a huge head of curly red hair and a single tear tattoo beneath his left eye.

"I went to school with Alex," Antonio said. "He was scary even as a teenager."

"Prairie City police would like its residents to be vigilant and keep their doors locked."

"Super"—I threw my hands in the air—"If that's it, can we see what happened at the end of the game?" I was practically shouting at the television.

"Boy Boy is thought to be armed and dangerous. If you spot him or have any information, please contact Prairie City PD."

They listed off a phone number before saying, "Now we'll head back to the Broncos-Raiders game where the Broncos have just caught the winning touchdown."

The screen flashed to a sea of orange and blue flooding the field where a pretty blonde sportscaster interviewed the players.

"Of course they won, and I missed it." I snapped the TV off.

"I'm sure we can catch a replay at the bar tonight," Shayla said apologetically.

"Ooh, the bar. Would you like some company?" Antonio asked.

"No," I said more harshly than I had intended. "I mean, I think it's a girls' night. Sorry."

Antonio looked genuinely hurt.

"Maybe next time?" Shayla offered, and he smiled a bit. "I'll be there right after my shift," she said to me.

I nodded. "I'll see you there after a bit."

I wore a pair of casual jeans, a white ribbed tank, and a Denver Broncos hoodie. I swiped several coats of mascara over my lashes, pulled my towel-dried hair into a messy bun, and re-wrapped my hand though the bite marks were already starting to heal.

It wasn't perfect, but I wasn't looking to impress anyone . . . especially at the local wing joint.

It wasn't as if the perfect man would appear out of nowhere and whisk me off my feet. That was the stuff of my childhood dreams. Okay, and maybe my teenage dreams too. But I was an adult now. I didn't believe in that stuff. Much.

"Rylie?" Mom called down the stairs. "Are you about ready for dinner?" I could already hear the commotion of my sister's four young boys running laps through the kitchen, the living room, and the dining room overhead.

"Yep," I called back and yanked on my Adidas.

Fizzy, my pit bull Lab mix, bounded up the stairs ahead of me and crashed into a tall and breathtakingly gorgeous man.

Luke.

That explained the smell of cookies and lasagna. I should have known.

"Fizzy, get down," I said, my voice barely audible over Luke's deep laugh and the boys' squeals of delight.

"Rylie, can you please get control of your dog?" Megan yelled, as if my dog was any more of a problem than her four little tornadoes.

"Fizzy, off." He obeyed and came to sit at my side.

Mom patted Fizzy on the head and then smoothed the collar of Luke's blue button down shirt while she batted her eyelashes shamelessly. "I'm glad you were able to join us, Luke. Rylie was *so* excited when I told her you were coming."

That little liar. She never told me he was coming. If she had, I wouldn't be here. I shot daggers from my eyes hoping she'd feel my wrath.

"She was, was she?" Luke asked not looking at me. I hadn't seen him in more than a month, and yet he managed to look a hundred times better than he did in my dreams. Not that I dreamed about him . . .

"It's six o'clock, let's eat." My father stood from his leather recliner in the living room and made his way to the formal dining room—the only room with a table large enough to cater to our entire family plus Luke.

"What happened to your hand?" Luke asked me as Mom dished us each up large helpings of deliciously thick noodles, gooey cheese, and homemade marinara sauce.

I looked down. "Snake bite."

Mom dropped my father's plate in front of him with a loud thud. "A snake bite?" she shrieked as Dad wiped off the sauce that had flown from the plate onto his green golf shirt. "Do you go out of your way to try and get your-self killed?"

"It was only a bullsnake. Not venomous." I assured her.

"Good thing it wasn't a rattler," Dad said with a smile. "When I was a boy we had a dog, Angus, who would kill rattlers out on the family farm. He could tell the differ-ence between the rattlers and the bullsnakes. He wouldn't get suckered by the bullsnakes' antics or into thinking the rattlers were harmless."

Perfect, a dog was smarter than me. I looked down where Fizzy lay quietly at my feet. He may not have been a snake hunter, but he was good at weeding out the human snakes. He had never liked Troy, my ex-boyfriend.

"The bullsnakes were the good ones. They kept the rodents away, and if they bit the livestock it wouldn't kill them, so we kept them around. But good old Angus, he'd grab those rattlers up in his mouth, give them a good shake, and drop them to the ground dead."

Dad was a master storyteller. Something about his tone of voice engaged even the most rambunctious boys.

"One time we were out on a walk, and he found one hissing away in the grass. He picked up that snake and shook it limp, but instead of dropping it he threw it at me." His voice boomed. "Wouldn't you know it, the snake —dead as a doornail—wrapped itself around my legs."

Mom let out a gasp. The boys were on the edges of their seats. I could imagine Dad's face looking something like what Seamus's had when I'd thrown the snake at his feet.

"What'd you do Grandpa?" The oldest boy asked.

"After nearly soiling myself, I untangled my legs and ran all the way back home."

"Did your dog still catch rattlesnakes?" I asked.

"Until the day he died." Dad's eyes hazed in remembrance, his mouth opening into a smile. "But thankfully he didn't throw another one at me. I was lucky the fangs didn't catch my skin, after all, since rattlers are still venomous after death."

Venomous after death sounded like the name of a punk band.

We all sat in silence for a moment, taking in the details of Dad's story and the warmth of Mom's lasagna.

"So Luke," Tom, Megan's husband, spoke up. "How are things on the force?"

Tom's construction company's work was far different than Luke's as a police officer.

"Not as exciting as they were earlier this summer," Luke replied, his ease with my family gave me an irritated sense of happiness deep in my stomach.

A month ago he and I had worked together on a murder investigation. Usually, park rangers, especially summer park rangers, didn't work on murder investigations. But since I was one of the rangers who found the body, I was happy to help. That is until it almost got me killed.

"Perhaps you and Rylie should find another body to investigate together," Mom said.

"I'm sorry, what?" Megan sputtered, nearly spitting out her wine.

"I meant a dead body, Megan." Mom's face turned a deep shade of red. "Get your head out of the gutter."

I fought the urge to laugh at my mother's expense. It would do no good to hurt her feelings.

"How is a dead body any better? Are you hoping someone dies so Rylie will get her chance with Luke again?" Megan asked, her words coming between bursts of laughter.

"Megan!" I elbowed her in the ribs and glanced up at Luke who seemed mildly amused.

"What? It's obvious what Mom is doing. Why else would she have invited Luke to join us for dinner?"

She was right, of course.

"Enough girls," my dad said in his kind voice. "I'm sure your mother didn't mean she wants anyone to die."

Always the peacemaker. Mom shot Dad a thankful glance, and he smiled back at her. How had they managed to stay married and in love for so long?

"It *has* been rather dull without wondering what kind of trouble Rylie would be getting into next," Luke said glancing up at me, his gaze flickering between my face and my neck. "Almost makes me hope for another dead body."

Both Mom and Megan let out audible sighs.

I fought the urge to stick my tongue out at him. Who in their right mind hoped for dead bodies?

"I have to go." I stood from the table too quickly, nearly toppling my chair. "I promised Shayla I'd meet her."

"Tell her I say hi," Luke said.

I nodded. "Sure."

"But can't you?" Mom began, but I was out the door before I could hear her complete her objection.

Shayla wore tight jeans with more confidence than I'd ever seen. Her light hair was pulled into a bun like mine, and her face held more makeup than a trip to the wings joint warranted.

"You look pretty. What's the occasion?" I asked taking my seat at the bar next to her. There weren't nearly as many people crowded around as there would be when second shift got off and all the local police officers came in to wind down.

"I have to find some way to compete with you," Shayla said blushing. "Plus, I went down another pant size today, and I felt especially pretty."

Shayla had been losing weight since she'd become a summie. Her goal was to make it into the police academy and follow in her mother and grandmother's footsteps.

"There's no competition. It's not like we even like the same guys. Well, anymore."

Shayla and I both laughed.

When we had first met, Shayla had a huge thing for Luke, but it seemed to have faded.

"I meant to ask before but how was your shift on the trails the other day? I'm doing my first trail shift tomorrow."

"It was pretty boring." She shrugged. "Dusty and I drove around for hours. We didn't see a single homeless person, rattlesnake, or drug dealer."

"Were you hoping to?" I took a swig of the beer the bartender handed me with a wink. Maybe I'd been coming here too often.

"I don't know, sorta, yeah. Mom thinks being a ranger is weak. If I had something exciting happen, maybe she'd take it more seriously. Take *me* more seriously."

Her mom was a complete and total jerk-wad. "Maybe next shift?"

Shayla raised her beer. "To more interesting shifts to come."

"Hear hear." I tapped her glass with mine and took another pull. "You'll never guess who my mother invited to dinner tonight."

Shayla shrugged. "Peyton Elway?"

"No not *Peyton Elway*." I sighed. I had been trying to teach her about football, but my efforts had been futile. "Peyton Elway isn't even a person. Luke."

"Of course she invited Luke." Shayla shook her head with a grin.

"I hadn't seen him since we'd solved the murder." I glanced up at the TV showing highlights from the Broncos game. "He looks good."

"When hasn't he looked good?" Shayla smiled. "I think you might be out of luck, though. From what I hear, he's been hanging out with Nikki a lot."

Ugh, that was precisely what I hadn't wanted to hear. I guess he wasn't waiting for me to get past my rebound stage like I thought he might.

"Speaking of . . ." Shayla nodded towards the door, and sure enough Luke and Nikki came waltzing in, arm in arm.

Had he seriously left my parents' house to go on a date with her?

17

"Let's go somewhere else." I downed the rest of my beer and slapped a five on the counter.

Shayla did the same as we both stood to leave.

"Leaving so soon?" The voice of a thousand fingernails raking against a chalkboard sent chills down my spine. It took everything in me not to turn and wrap my hands around her skinny little perfect neck and—

"This place is a dud tonight." Shayla took a step between Nikki and me.

I dared a glance up into Luke's eyes, which seemed vaguely apologetic. Or was that pity? It didn't matter because Shayla was pulling me out the door.

"Can you believe they came here?" I asked when we were outside in the fresh air.

"It was kind of Luke's place before it was ours."

"Whatever. I need to find a man. I need to get past this rebound stigma." Before Nikki had her claws so far into Luke that I couldn't remove them.

3

"Tinder or eHarmony?" I asked sitting at the second bar of the night.

"I'd go with Tinder. Less intense." Shayla sat down and ordered us a couple of beers.

"Okay, Tinder downloaded." I looked up from my phone. "Now what?"

"You need a good picture. The one from your Facebook is okay, but . . ."

I knew what she was saying. A picture of Fizzy and me sticking our tongues out at the camera would likely attract the wrong kind of attention.

"Do you have any selfies?"

"Uh? Without Fizzy?" I scrolled through my pictures. "Doesn't look like it."

"Okay, I'll take a picture of you. Hold still." Shayla snapped a photo and held it out for me to see. "It's pretty good."

If pretty good meant a hot mess, she was right. Ugh. "It'll do."

"Now you need to come up with a short description of yourself." She handed the phone back to me.

What was I going to say? Broke, living in my parent's basement, bested by rattlesnake wannabes, oh but I can solve a murder without being killed . . . barely. Yeah, I didn't think so. "I don't know, Shayla, maybe this isn't a good idea. Don't you think I could just pick someone up at a bar or something?"

"Nobody does that anymore. It's like you've been out of the dating game since high school."

I practically had. "Then you write something. I don't know what to say."

She thought about it for a few seconds and then began typing furiously. She was way more versed in these things being several years younger than me. "There. That should do it." Her smile was nothing short of evil genius.

I squinted down at the screen.

Park Ranger seeking someone who can keep up. I'm a badass and super hot. I like light beer with lime and long walks up steep mountains. I have a dog. If you're allergic, swipe left.

I nearly peed my pants. "Shayla, I can't say those things."

"That's nothing. Wait until you see what other people write."

"But I'm not a badass and definitely not super hot."

"Um, not that I'm into that sort of thing, but have you looked in the mirror lately?"

I blushed. "What does swipe left mean?"

"To bug off." She giggled. "Or that they don't like you. You do the same. See?"

She went to all the guys I'd been paired with. "See this guy? Says he's just in it for some fun. Um, left."

"But he was kinda cute."

"Fun means sex. He wants a bootie call."

I could feel my jaw drop. "What self-respecting woman would swipe right for that?"

Shayla's cheeks flushed. She slowly raised her hand.

"No. Way." I shook my head. "Shayla, what would have made you . . ."

"It had been a long time, and I thought it might be a good idea. I didn't go through with it."

That's when the laughter commenced. "I. . . cannot . . . believe," I said through gasps. "You . . . could . . . have . . . gotten . . . *herpes!*"

We both laughed harder at the last word. Shayla's face lit up when she laughed. It was a bummer she thought she had to stoop to that level to get the attention of a man.

"So have you met anyone of any worth doing this?" I asked when we had finally composed ourselves.

"Not really, but I haven't been on very long." She shrugged. "What's the worst that could happen?"

By two in the morning, I had gone through each and every guy the app considered a match for me. I only swiped right on a few—the ones that weren't too cringeworthy.

Shayla promised I'd get more matches as time went on, so even if I didn't find someone right away it could still happen. I finally had to put the phone down to get some much-needed rest before my trail shift. I was shadowing Seamus, and I wanted to be as prepared as possible. He'd already seen me make an idiot of myself with that snake. I didn't want him to think me completely incapable of doing my job. Especially if he had any say in who would get the full-time position.

The trail rangers, though technically park rangers, didn't typically patrol the reservoirs but rather the many miles of trails throughout Prairie City—one of the largest cities in northern Colorado. Their office was located several miles from where I'd been stationed all summer at Alder Ridge Reservoir. If I got the full-time position, I'd get to patrol all three of the reservoirs, maybe the trails, and possibly even the open space areas that were disbursed between neighborhoods and that butted up to the foothills.

I typed the trail ranger office address into my GPS making sure I could hit a Starbucks on the way. After getting only three hours of sleep, I was going to need a quadruple shot of espresso.

Seamus leaned against the side of his truck sipping his coffee when I arrived. He had on aviators even though the sun hadn't risen. The building behind him was dark, but I could see two garage doors and what looked to be a small office area attached. Not as nice as the shop at the reservoir, but not too shabby.

"Good morning," I said in my most enthusiastic voice.

"Nope." He held out his hand stopping me in my tracks. "Rule number one. Don't talk until my coffee cup is empty." His Irish accent was almost endearing enough to think he was joking, but his face told a much more serious story.

"Okay"

"Not a word. And stop smilin' so big, it's hurtin' my eyes." He motioned to the truck. "Get in."

I loaded my bag into the back seat and took my spot as passenger. I only made it two minutes before the urge to speak started bubbling up inside me like a shaken bottle of root beer.

I shifted in my seat. How could he be so quiet? Just sitting there slowly sipping his coffee, driving down the road.

I couldn't take it anymore.

"I joined Tinder last night."

Seriously? That's the first thing to come out of my mouth?

Seamus moved his glasses down his nose and looked at me over them, his deep blue eyes both terrifying and mysterious. "Three minutes." His mouth widened into a grin. "Benny was right. Yeh are a talker."

I let out a nervous laugh as he retrained his gaze onto the road in front of us.

"Tinder, huh? Is that what the cool kids do these days?"

"I guess so. Sorry, I didn't mean to blurt that out."

"Yeh can't take it back now, Blondie." He laughed like the adorable leprechaun on the cereal commercials. "Why would a gal like you need to go on such a site?"

I didn't even know this guy's brand of coffee, and we were already talking about my love life. Good one, Rylie. "I guess it's hard to find someone at my age."

"At yer age? What are yeh, a whole twenty-two?"

"Twenty-eight, thank you very much. And I don't mean because I'm old. I mean because I'm young. Apparently, everyone my age is on Tinder."

"That's because yer generation's full of wussy men."

It was my turn to laugh. He had a point.

"Since when do these *men* not know how to pick up a girl at a bar like the rest of us?" He turned off the main road and drove down a sidewalk expertly dodging the bollard installed to prevent that sort of action.

"That's what I said too, but Shayla said"

"Shayla, huh? How many men has Shayla met on this Tinder thingy?" Man, for someone who didn't want me to talk until his coffee was gone, he sure was chatty.

"I don't know, some."

He shrugged. "I guess it's worth a shot. Let me know how that goes for yeh."

Yeah, no. I'd be perfectly happy leaving my personal dating life out of our future conversations. "So where are we going?"

"I'm going to give yeh a brief overview of the trail system in the city. We obviously can't hit everything in one day, but this'll give yeh an idea of what a trail ranger does."

"How often do the park rangers go on trail patrol?"

"Not often enough. There's only two of us for all these trails. The most common time is in the winter when the parks are slow." He took a left at a Y in the trail and headed underneath an overpass. "I wouldn't recommend coming here alone when the sun's down especially since yeh summies don't have the Kevlar." He knocked on his chest where a bulletproof vest rested beneath his uniform shirt. "As yeh can see, there are some hooligans who hang out down in these parts."

Several homeless tents were set up under the bridge.

"Do we do anything with them?"

"We can put notices on their tents and tell them to leave. We can even take their belongings if they don't heed our warnings. But if they're not hurtin' anything, I like to leave 'em be. Dusty, on the other hand, thinks it's his personal mission to rid the world of homelessness."

"So he takes their things?"

"After he makes sure they have a place to stay and a hot meal. He's a big softie behind his body builder look."

Though Seamus himself wasn't terrible to look at, Dusty was even more handsome. Where Seamus was shorter and scruffier, Dusty was tall and built with smooth chocolate skin.

I nodded.

"He's got a girl, in case yeh was wonderin'."

"I don't date guys I work with."

Seamus let out another cheerful laugh. "That's what they all say. Yeh've met Antonio, right?"

"Antonio is married." And Italian and gorgeous.

"Marriage is more of a suggestion in Antonio's world."

"Well, I think marriage should be a serious

commitment."

"Sounds like yeh should have joined eHarmony instead."

I lifted an eyebrow. "It sounds like you know more about these dating sites than you let on."

He shrugged. "Gotta keep up with the times there, Blondie." He took a sip of his coffee. "But I have to say, I find it rather presumptive to describe yerself as badass and super hot."

"How do you know that's what my profile says?"

"Don't worry. I swiped left." His voice was completely nonchalant as if it wasn't weird we'd been matched in the first place.

It wasn't that he wasn't attractive, he just wasn't my type. I liked guys to be at least a few inches taller than me.

"Over there yeh'll see one of our intercity ponds, Golden Rock." A pond almost as large as a football field lay below what promised to be a breathtaking sunrise breaking over the distant mountains. "Here take these," he produced a pair of binoculars from his bag in the back seat of the truck, "and tell me what yeh see. Describe everything."

I adjusted the lenses carefully to fit my eyes. "I see three fishermen standing shoulder to shoulder on the west bank. They look to be in their sixties. Next to the one furthest to the right are a cooler, a Thermos, and a fold-up chair that looks to have an American flag printed on it."

"Dusty and I call them the three amigos. They're almost always fishing here at sun up. Go on."

I searched slowly around the perimeter of the pond, "A

flock of geese just landed on the north side and . . . there's a boat." I adjusted the binoculars to focus more closely. "It's a small boat with an electric motor, and there are two men fishing. I can't see their faces, but they look to be around the same size."

I searched for anything else of note, but nothing popped up. "I think that's it."

"Okay," he held his hand out for the binoculars, "Let me have a go."

It was too early in the morning for a test. But at least we weren't talking about my love life anymore.

"I see the three amigos. They seem to be at their usual antics. Though there is more around them than a cooler, a thermos, and a chair. They also have tackle boxes and poles with them." He glanced over at me. "Don't worry. It's early."

I tried not to roll my eyes. Of course they had tackle boxes and fishing poles, what fisherman didn't?

"As far as the geese, yep, they're definitely there." He scanned further. "And the boat . . . wait . . . how many fishermen did yeh say were in the boat?"

"Two."

"Take another look," he handed the binoculars back to me.

Upon second glance, I could only make out the profile of one fisherman. I watched a bit longer. Maybe the other was leaning down to prepare his line, but after several minutes nothing changed. "I know there were two before."

"There is definitely only one person in that boat." His tone was teasing, and a grin spread over his face. "Maybe yeh need more coffee and less Tinder if you're starting to conjure up men in your head."

"No, I'm serious. There were two men in that boat." A warning blared in my head. "What if one pushed the other out or something?" A man could be drowning out there, and Seamus was making a joke about it.

"Calm down, Blondie. I'm sure it was just the sunrise shadows playing tricks on yer eyes. I know yeh came in blazin' with a murder on yer first day, but those things don't happen very often. Yeh can't go makin' a big deal out of every little thing."

"Can I see again?" I asked holding my hand out. Surely there had to be an explanation.

He obliged and handed the binoculars over. By now the sun was starting to peek up over the mountains and rays of sunlight made it harder and harder to see the details of the boat. "I know I saw two figures. They looked almost identical," I murmured under my breath.

"Maybe it was a reflection in the binoculars. You only saw them for a few seconds."

The single figure was reeling in his line. The water surrounding him was totally calm—no sign of someone drowning.

"Can we at least go over there and check it out?" I asked. The man was now heading back to the boat ramp.

"If it'll soothe yer mind, sure." Seamus smiled. "But I'm pretty sure I'm not going to rely on yeh to give me detailed information in the future." He nudged my arm, and I glared at him. "I'm kiddin'. I'm kiddin'." He pushed his aviators back on his face as if he were Tom Cruise in Top Gun and put the truck in gear.

The three amigos waved when we drove by, their identical white mustaches twitching upward into smiles. "They're good guys. Retired vets."

I nodded, trying to focus on what Seamus was saying, but finding it hard over the pounding of my heart. The water where the boat had previously been anchored was still calm, and the fisherman was loading the boat onto a trailer when we pulled up.

"Let me do the talking." He stepped out of the truck before I could respond. "Hey there. How was the fishing this morning?"

"Not bad. Caught a few little trout. Threw 'em all back." The man was huge. He towered over my five foot eight frame, and his bicep was probably as big as my head. "Anyone else have any luck?"

"Couldn't say. Haven't talked to anyone else. Could I see yer fishing license?"

"Oh sure." He pulled out his tackle box and produced a folded blue piece of paper. The inside of the tackle box was far from orderly with tangled lures, crusty jars of sticky marshmallow bait, and a few prescription drug bottles.

"Thank you, Garrett." Seamus handed the license back. Garrett tossed it in with the rest of the mess, slammed the lid shut, and dropped the box back into his boat next to a large black duffle bag.

"Do I know you from somewhere?" Garrett asked. I tore my eyes from the contents of the boat and focused on the bearded man in front of me. He had to be in his early thirties.

My thoughts whirled. Did I know him?

"Oh, no way," the guy's mouth curled into a smile, "You're the badass ranger on Tinder." He looked me up and down. "Your profile wasn't lying. I kinda wish I would've swiped right." He let out a low whistle.

I didn't know whether to be flattered or embarrassed. It wasn't that he wasn't handsome—he definitely was—but his cocky attitude was a bit off-putting.

Seamus let out a bray like that of an ass, which was exactly what I wanted to call him at that very moment.

"Were you fishing alone?" I blurted out, my hands on my hips.

The guy mimicked my stance. "Yes, but next time you can come with me."

Classic deflection. "That's not why I was—"

"We'll let yeh get on with yer day," Seamus grabbed me by the crook of my arm and pulled me back to the truck.

"Let me give you my number," Garrett said.

Seamus dropped my arm and walked back.

No.

He wouldn't.

I spun around to see Seamus take a business card Garrett had pulled from the back pocket of his ripped jeans.

"Call me. We'll get a drink," Garrett said with a wink.

Yeah, not likely.

"I cannot believe you just did that," I said as Seamus handed me the card.

"It's the least I could do after yeh were so mean to the guy," Seamus said when we were securely within the truck. "If yeh want to be a trail ranger, yeh need to be cool, calm, and collected. We don't get our panties in a bunch and go around asking stupid questions."

"Did you see the extra rods in his boat? And the jacket and boots?" I threw back at him. "He wasn't fishing alone."

"Most fishermen carry enough gear for several people." He started back down the trail away from the boat launch area. "Plus I don't think that boat could have handled two men his size and you did say both men were the same build."

I held in the groan threatening to escape my lips. The boat *had* been rather wimpy, but I knew what I saw . . . At least I thought I did. "He was deflecting. That whole Tinder thing, maybe he was using it to distract us from what was really going on."

"There was nothin' going on. Other than a guy trying to make a pass at yeh. Maybe *that's* yer problem, yeh're too suspicious to get a date." He looked down at the card in my hand. "Senior Accountant, huh? I'd call him if I were into dudes."

The business card gave his name as Garrett Henry and an office number in the ritzy part of town, a cell number, and an email address that contained his first and last name. Maybe I should update my email address from the one I'd had since high school. The one that described my hair color and old zip code. I shook the thought away.

"But what about the prescription drugs in his tackle box?"

"Could be for anything. Though I'd be careful dating him. He might have the clap or something."

"I am *not* going to date him," I said through gritted teeth. "Did you see how messy he was?"

"Okay, okay. But don't judge a guy on the state of his fishing gear. If yeh did that, yeh'd never date anyone."

Seamus was apparently not going to take me seriously. I tried to calm my pounding heart. The water was still motionless. If someone had been pushed out of the boat, they'd have drowned by now. I looked back at the pond one more time before we turned down another trail and the pond disappeared from sight.

I turned the business card over in my hand. Senior Accountant. He didn't seem like the accountant type to me. His hair was too long, his beard unkempt. Every accountant I'd met was clean shaven and wore glasses.

"Let's head over to the playground and check to see if anyone's taken up residence in the restroom. Then maybe we'll do some snake handling drills. If yeh want to get the full-time position, yeh'll need to work on taming the slithery beasts." Seamus maneuvered the truck down the winding pathway with million dollar houses to our left and a creek to our right. "The people in these houses are always watching. Regardless of what yeh do on this path, the higher-ups will know."

"Why even come down this path then?" I glanced over to find a man who was at least eighty on the back deck of one house and what looked like a middle-aged woman peeking from behind the curtains of another.

"Have to. They report if we're not here too." He waved to the peeping woman, and she quickly closed the curtains.

"What's that?" I pointed to what looked like it could

be a large dog lying in the middle of the concrete about twenty yards ahead.

"We better check it out." He pulled up closer and veered the truck off the concrete into the mowed shoulder. "Get out yer pepper spray, just in case."

I pulled the canister out and made sure I had it pointed the right way so I didn't accidentally spray myself if I needed to use it.

Seamus stepped out of the truck, and I followed. He readied his asp—a telescoping baton—as it was the best option between the two weapons the full-time rangers were allowed to carry—an asp and pepper spray.

"Hello?" Seamus said as he approached what I could now see was clearly not a dog. He poked at what looked like a fuzzy blanket covering something. "Yeh ready?"

I nodded and held the can in front of me taking aim.

Seamus stuck the end of his asp under the blanket and lifted.

It took a minute for my brain to register what my eyes were seeing but once they did, there was no unseeing it.

A small man, probably around the age of twenty, lay curled in a ball in a pool of what I assumed to be his blood.

"Bloody hell." Seamus let the blanket drop back over the body and called into his mic, "Yeah we got a code fifty-five at mile seven on the Golden Rock Trail."

"Copy, we'll send a unit," the dispatcher replied.

Seamus rubbed the back of his neck. He turned his attention to me. "Yeh's a right ol' shit magnet, Blondie."

4

T he police arrived within twenty minutes, and within thirty, Luke pulled up.

"Looks like your wish came true," I muttered so only he could hear.

"I didn't *really* want someone to die." Luke shook his head. "Tell me what happened."

"I'm not sure. It was my first trail patrol, and Seamus was showing me the ropes." I motioned to where Seamus talked with one of the officers. "We saw the three amigos down by Golden Rock Pond, a boat with one or two men —I couldn't say at this point."

Luke furrowed his brow, but I dismissed it with a wave.

"It was one . . . probably. Anyway, we were driving down this trail and came upon this heap. I thought it might be a dog." I pursed my lips looking to where one of the paramedics stood over the body shaking his head.

"Seamus used the tip of his asp to pull up the blanket, and when we saw the blood, he put the blanket back down and called you guys."

"Do you recognize the deceased?"

"I didn't get a good look at him." The look on Luke's face gave me pause. "Wait. Should I recognize him?"

"He was one of the people of interest in the Boy Boy escape."

"And now he's dead?"

My gaze darted to the area around us. Boy Boy could be anywhere just waiting to kill again.

"Does that mean . . ?"

"I need you to be careful, Ry. This guy's not like Kyle. He's a known killer. He'll do whatever's necessary to stay out of prison."

I nodded. "Don't worry. There's not even a small part of me that wants to help catch Boy Boy."

"Good." Luke moved as if to put his arm around me but stopped himself. "I should get back to the investigation."

My heart dropped. "Seamus and I should be getting back too. Shayla's probably waiting on me at the shop to work out."

"It's great you and Shayla have become so close. She needed a good friend."

"I needed one too."

Luke's brown eyes made me want to wrap my arms around his neck and nuzzle my cheek against his chest like I had so many times in high school.

"Sorry Nikki and I messed up your night last night."

And, in an instant, my warm and fuzzy feelings evaporated. "You didn't. We just thought we'd try a different place. Shayla set me up on Tinder which seems like it could work."

"Oh yeah?" Luke rocked back on his heels. "You've already met someone?"

"Yep." Kinda, if the fisherman counted. "He seems pretty great." And cocky. Someone who would give Luke a run for his money. Hmmm . . .

"Well, that's great." His tone didn't sound like he thought it was great. Before he could say anything else, his cell phone rang in his pocket. "I should probably—"

"Yeah, you get that. I'll see you later."

I thumbed the business card in my pocket. What would one little date hurt?

The first thing I did when my shift was over was pull up the Tinder app and look for Garrett's profile. I swiped and swiped and swiped but came up empty handed. It must have taken him out of my dating pool when he swiped left.

So instead I pulled up Facebook.

What little I could see of his profile seemed fairly normal. His profile picture looked like him minus the beard he'd been sporting this morning. And there weren't any random photos of him with other girls. At least not public ones.

I pulled out the business card and typed the cell

number into the new text message box. My thumb hovered over the screen. What would I say?

The last first date I had been on was over five years ago, with the man I'd found in my bed embracing a long-necked woman the same day I'd lost my job, and my world flipped upside down.

Hey Garrett, it's Rylie the park ranger. How about that drink?

I closed my eyes, held my breath, and tapped the send button.

Shayla texted me later that night.

another dead body

Ugh. Yes.

was Luke there

Yep.

you're not going to try to investigate this one, right

No way. Too dangerous.

good. how's the tinder hunt

I have a date tomorrow night.

is he cute

Above average.

perfect

I dropped my phone on the nightstand next to my bed and hugged Fizzy around the neck. Garrett had responded almost immediately asking me to dinner rather than drinks, and I replied with a 'yes' before I could talk myself out of it.

"So tell me everything."

Shayla and I had been scheduled to open the reservoir together. She held her travel coffee mug, and I held my Starbucks as we waited to open the gates until exactly 5:00 AM.

"Yesterday, I saw a boat with what I could swear was two guys in it"—I had to let that go—"but when Seamus looked through the binoculars there was only one. So we talked to the guy, and he recognized me from Tinder. Though he had already swiped left."

Shayla shook her head. "That's no big deal. It was probably an accident. And you hit it off?"

"Kinda. I guess." I really didn't want to tell her I had initially thought he had thrown someone overboard.

"But you agreed to go out with him?"

"Yeah, I mean, I figure he's cute enough, and I sorta told Luke I'd already found someone on Tinder."

"Luke." She shook her head. "Please tell me you're not going out with this guy to make Luke jealous?"

"Not completely." I smirked. "Who knows. Maybe Luke and I aren't meant to be together."

Shayla shrugged. "Seamus has taken to call you the shit magnet."

"I don't know whether that's better or worse than Blondie." I smiled. It was nice to be part of a team again. I missed the playful banter I'd had at the fire department.

"It's scary Boy Boy is on the loose," Shayla said.

"On the loose and murdering people, apparently."

"And you're going to keep your nose out of this one, right?"

I gave her an exasperated look. "Yes. I told you that last night."

"Just making sure you hadn't changed your mind."

"Boy Boy's not like Kyle. I'm not exactly equipped to handle him."

"You weren't exactly equipped to handle Kyle either. As I recall, you almost died."

I reached up letting my fingers brush over the scars on my neck. "Yes. But I didn't. And I don't intend on dying anytime soon."

"Good. Should we let the crazies in?" She motioned to the large wooden gates blocking the main entrance to the park and the line a half-mile long of cars and trucks holding eager fishermen.

I nodded, and we swung the gates open. A few hands waved from the windows, and some even hollered a good morning before they headed out to get their chances at catching the big one.

———

My shift passed quickly due to the busyness of the reservoir. There were fishermen everywhere just begging to have their licenses checked.

Okay, so maybe not begging.

In fact, some of them were downright irritated I'd checked their licenses for the 'millionth time' this month.

I was tempted to tell them to get another hobby, but instead I shrugged and reminded them I see a lot of fishermen and couldn't remember them all.

"I hear you have a date tonight," Antonio said when I pulled into the shop to refill my Starbucks cup with the coffee sludge resembling old motor oil.

"What's it to you?" I tipped the pot up and could have sworn a chunk fell into my cup.

Antonio leaned back against the wall giving me every opportunity to ogle his rugged Italian handsomeness. He even made the gray and navy uniforms look good. I took a sip of my coffee, and the bitterness brought me back to reality.

Married.

I shook my head.

"I want to make sure I won't have to save you again. This man, you know him?"

"I've met him once."

"In real life?"

"Yep." I shifted from one foot to another. I'd wring Shayla's neck for telling him all this.

"I hope he's worth it," Antonio continued as he followed me back out to my truck, "You are quite the catch, if I may use a fishing pun."

"Ugh, I wish you wouldn't." I pulled the door open and turned to find Antonio standing mere inches from me. He smelled like expensive Italian cologne—spicy and forbidden.

"My wife and I have separated." His voice was low and rumbly as his gaze bore into mine.

"That's, um—" I cleared my throat, "—nice." I took a step back, but there was nowhere else to go. My knees buckled, and my butt plopped down in the truck seat behind me.

"So maybe sometime we could . . ." He hovered over me now. Part of me wanted to slam the door on his head, but the other part wanted to reach up into his perfect hair and

"Ranger Sixteen, Ranger Fourteen," Brock, called on the radio. I let out a breath that was making me light headed. At least I was telling myself it was the lack of oxygen.

"Ranger Sixteen, Ranger Fourteen?" Brock's voice again.

"Ranger Fourteen, go ahead," I croaked out.

"I just wanted to let you know I'd be checking licenses on the dam."

"Copy." Why was he checking in with me when Antonio was the shift supervisor?

"Thanks, Sixteen clear."

"I'll let you think about it." Antonio turned and walked back into the shop.

Dammit.

5

I t took me entirely too long to decide on the black miniskirt and silver sequined one-shoulder top with my black stiletto heels. I curled my hair into loose waves and managed a great smoky eye before deciding that was as good as it was gonna get.

"Whoa, where are you going? To the club?" Megan teased as I headed out the door.

"Too much?"

"I don't know that too much is the appropriate term. Perhaps too little," my mother looked down at my legs. "I have a longer skirt you could borrow."

I bet she did. "Thanks. I'll be okay."

"Well, don't let your father see you like that." She shook her head.

"You look great," Megan said when Mom was out of earshot.

Meli's Margaritas was completely packed when I arrived. I parked Cherry Anne—my red Ford Mustang—in the back of the lot and cursed every step I took in the dreaded heels. Hopefully, I wouldn't catch a crack in the pavement and fall on my face. Road rash definitely wouldn't go with this outfit.

The restaurant had opened for business last month and was nearly impossible to get into. The frosted glass doors opened into a bar where people milled around looking expensive sipping from their huge margarita glasses. The décor was that of a typical Mexican restaurant only hipper with its twinkling lights and upscale furniture.

"Rylie?" A man at the bar turned and nearly fell off his stool. Two empty margarita glasses sat on the bar in front of him.

"Garrett. It's nice to see you."

"Wow, you're even hotter" a drunk hiccup burst from his mouth, "In person."

"You mean out of uniform?" I corrected.

"Yeah. Exactly." He blushed. His deep blue eyes sparkled like the water just before the sun rose over the reservoir. "I think I've had too much to drink. I'm sorry."

Drunk guys were usually a total turn-off, but Garrett seemed nicer, humbler as a drunk than he had sober. "It's okay. Should we get a table?"

"Absolutely." He spoke to the hostess, reminding her of our reservation and we were seated almost instantly.

The further we ventured into the restaurant, the more immersive the experience. The atmosphere darkened slightly, only lit by tiny twinkle lights hovering over the tables. The smoky smell of sizzling fajitas made my mouth water while the sound of a live band reminded me of the trip to Costa Rica my senior year of high school.

"Here you go." The hostess stopped at a cozy booth in the corner of the room, her eyes glued to my face.

"Thanks." I took the menu, but she didn't leave.

"I'm sorry, this is totally unprofessional," she pulled out her phone, "But are you the girl from the video?"

"What video?" I shifted in my seat. "I don't think I've been in any videos lately."

Garrett gave me a kind smile. They probably got bigwigs in here all the time, but I definitely wasn't one of them.

"Oh," her face fell a bit. "I thought you might be that ranger who was attacked by the snake and sat on a little girl's sand castle."

The air around me seemed to thin making it hard to suck in a breath. "Were you there?"

"No, I saw it on YouTube." She tapped a few buttons on her phone and turned it to face me. "You're going viral."

I yanked the phone closer. It was me. Falling, being bitten, throwing the snake on repeat. "No. No no no," I said under my breath.

My voice was shouting at Seamus, "I'm only dying over here," was expertly woven into the background music and the sounds of the crowd's laughter.

I examined the video more closely. I really needed to do something about my hair. My roots were starting to show.

"It *is* you!" The waitress let out a squeal. "I can't believe you're here. How's your hand?"

Garrett looked back and forth between the two of us, a confused smile plastered on his face.

"My hand's fine." I looked down at the two puncture marks that were healing nicely.

"Is this your boyfriend?"

"Um, no," I replied. "We're on our first date."

"We met on Tinder," Garrett blurted out. "Kinda."

"Tinder? Girl, with those legs and your newfound fame —even if it's bad fame—you don't need to go on Tinder."

"Well, thanks, but—"

"I'm sorry. I'll let you get on with your date." She slid her phone back into her pocket. "Can I get you anything to drink?"

"I'll take a margarita," Garrett said almost too quickly.

"I'll have an ice tea." Drinking on the first date didn't seem like a great idea, especially a first date with a man who was already drunk off his ass.

"Sorry about that," I said when the hostess left.

"It's okay." Garrett wiped a bead of sweat from his forehead. "You know we don't have to do this if you don't want to."

"Of course I want to," I said, only half lying.

"Because I know you're a catch. I still can't believe you texted me."

I shrugged. Where was the cocky guy from the park? "I figured I'd give you a chance."

He nodded. "Sorry about the snake video. I'm glad your hand is okay."

"Thanks."

"Here are your drinks," the hostess said. "Would you

mind signing this for me?" She pulled out a napkin with the restaurant's logo on it.

She had to be joking. I looked up expecting her to laugh, but instead, she pushed her pen towards my face.

"Sure," I signed it quickly, and she bounded away from the table tucking the napkin safely into her pocket.

"It's too bad people don't want my autograph for something more—I don't know—positive."

Garrett had already gulped down half of his margarita. "If you weren't so beautiful, no one would care."

I doubted they were checking me out. But it was a nice compliment. "So you're an accountant?"

He nodded. "It's a good gig. Several of the Broncos players are clients. Are you a fan?"

"Isn't everyone?"

"Seems like it." He took another sip of his margarita. "I have tickets for this weekend's home game if you'd like to go."

I tried to keep my face as neutral as possible while my insides squealed yes, yes, say yes! Which was worse that he was actually asking me out again after we were only ten minutes into our date, or that I was only too willing to say yes?

"Sure," I finally replied. Hopefully, he wasn't too drunk to remember this conversation. I'd never been to an actual game.

"Cool." He smiled and seemed to relax a bit. "So, have you met a lot of people on Tinder?"

"You're the first, uh, well sort of, I guess." I laughed. "A friend of mine convinced me to set up the profile."

"Me too. I didn't have much interest, but I thought why not? Most of the women I'm interested in swipe left."

Why would any woman swipe left? He was tall and built and handsome. Maybe his profile was a booty call.

I glanced across the table to see him take a sip of his drink only to have it dribble down his chin. Maybe it was because behind the outward appearance, this guy was a verifiable lush, though how they could figured that out from a simple Tinder profile was beyond me.

It didn't take long to order and receive our food—steak fajitas for me and an enormous quesadilla for him. The waiter looked at me with a knowing grin but thankfully didn't say anything about the video.

Just as we were getting ready to leave and Garrett was signing the credit card slip, a familiar face caught my eye. Nikki. And Luke. Sitting across the restaurant.

They were talking about something that looked rather intense. Either that or Nikki's stick had traveled further up her ass.

My stare must have borne a hole in Luke's back because he turned to glance over at our booth. I looked away before he caught me staring. Before I could talk myself out of it, I reached across and touched Garrett's arm giggling as if he had told the funniest joke in the world.

He let out a confused laugh. "Did I say something?" His speech even more slurred now that he'd finished his fourth enormous margarita—the limit for how many the restaurant would serve one person.

"You're just so cute," I said with a smile knowing full well Luke was watching. "Should we head out?"

His head bobbed. "Definitely."

We stood from the booth, me doing my best to show-case my legs and the shortness of my skirt and him trying not to fall over. I hooked my arm in his, thankful he was steady enough to support most of his own weight and did my best love-to-watch-her-go walk hoping Luke was taking it all in.

"Where'd you park?" I asked when we got to the parking lot.

"Uh, I think . . ." he glanced around not seeming to comprehend my question entirely.

I couldn't let him drive himself, not like this.

"How about I drive you home?" I asked.

He nodded. "Thanks."

It took double the time getting back to my car. Between my heels and him practically falling all over me, I was surprised we made it there at all. Part of me hoped he would forget inviting me to the Broncos game after all. I didn't mind a guy who had an occasional beer now and then, but I hated a sloppy drunk.

Thankfully he stayed conscious long enough to give me his address before passing out in my passenger seat. I silently willed him not to barf on Cherry Anne's leather.

His house was a swanky brick two story with a double garage underneath part of the main living quarters in one of the wealthy parts of town. Accountants did rather well for themselves.

"Garrett?" I said when we pulled up to the curb.

"Huh?" He opened his eyes and wiped the drool coming from the corner of his mouth. "We're here already?"

"Yep."

He reached for the door handle and managed to get himself out of the car and up to his front steps. I followed. "Do you mind if I use your bathroom before I leave?" I asked.

"Not at all," he fumbled with the keys before finally resting on one and unlocking the door. "Hey, Babbitt. Good boy." He reached down and patted the head of an adorable husky. "This is Rylie. Can you say hello?"

Babbitt let out a loud yowl.

I bent down and scratched him under the chin. "Hello Babbitt, it's a pleasure to meet you." He responded with a big kiss.

"The bathroom's right through there," Garrett pointed down the hallway and then flopped down on the plush leather sofa, Babbitt coming to rest on the floor next to him.

The inside of his home was completely opposite from what I had expected. It was spotless. Decorated in the latest décor, it looked like a page out of Modern Homes Magazine. The only personal photos were of him with Babbitt and various children—likely the nieces and nephews he'd raved about at dinner.

Hardwood floors stretched throughout the open concept living room and kitchen and led to a set of stairs up to the second story of the house, a few closed doors, which probably led to bedrooms, and a door to the garage.

The bathroom was pristine. I opened the medicine cabinet as quietly as possible to find absolutely nothing. Not one single bottle of any sort, prescription or not.

Where were the bottles I'd seen in his tackle box?

Maybe they were still in the tackle box. Or in the master bathroom.

I closed the cabinet door.

What was I doing? Seamus was right. I was looking for trouble that wasn't even there.

When I emerged from the bathroom, I stopped to watch Garrett play with Babbitt. He would tell Babbitt to stay, and Babbitt would stay still as a statue until Garrett said, "Sick," and Babbitt would attack the plush toy duck on the floor.

"Did you find it okay?" he mumbled when I walked over to the couch.

"Yeah," I said. "Thanks for dinner. I should probably be going."

"You're not going to go to the Broncos game with me are you?"

"Uh," I contemplated whether to be honest or not. Part of me really wanted to go to the game, but dating shouldn't feel like babysitting my four-year-old nephew.

"Don't worry about it. I understand." His eyes were closed with one of his arms draped over his forehead.

I sat down on the edge of the couch and scratched Babbitt behind the ears. "Are you going to be okay tonight by yourself?"

"I'll be fine. I've got Babbitt," he said. I went to stand, but he gently grabbed my hand—his palm as smooth as a brand new tub of butter. "I'm sorry I messed up our date. I guess I got nervous to go out with someone as cool as you."

"I'm not that cool," I said.

His big blue eyes focused on my face, a smile breached his lips. "Yes. You are."

I returned his grin.

"Will you at least sleep on it before you completely turn me down for the Broncos game?"

I thought about it for a couple of seconds. What was the worst that could happen if I went on another date with him? He'd get drunk again and I'd call him an Uber? At least I'd get to see the game in person.

"You know what? I don't have to sleep on it." I squeezed his hand. "I'll go to the game with you."

"You won't regret it." He rubbed his thumb over mine sending shivers up my arm. "And I promise not to get plastered."

"Deal."

6

"Rylie?" My mother's voice and a tap at my door woke me five minutes before my alarm was supposed to go off. Five precious minutes of sleep gone.

"What, Mom?"

She opened the door as if my response was an invitation to come in.

"I wanted to make sure you got home alive."

She'd waited long enough. If something had happened the night before, my body would be cold and stiff by now.

"Thanks for checking in," I mumbled from under my pillow. "I'm good,"

"You know, I don't think it's a good idea for you to go on dates with men you've only met on the Internet. There's this thing called catfishing, and it sounds dangerous—especially after what happened at the reservoir when you started there."

I pulled the pillow off my head and reminded myself

she was only trying to look out for my best interests. "Mom, catfishing, in the dating sense, is when someone acts like they're someone else. They never actually meet you in person because they're not real. I'm in no danger of being catfished."

"Okay maybe not that, but still, those men seem to be after only one thing . . ."

One thing I hadn't had in months. "I'll be careful. I promise."

She exhaled, voicing her dissatisfaction with my response more than the pained look on her face and stood up. "Have a great day."

"Thanks. You too."

The moment the door clicked into place behind her my alarm clock blared notifying me that sleep was another many hours away. Fizzy groaned.

"Me too, bud." I patted his head and rolled out from under the covers.

———

I pulled into the shop parking lot and took the last sip of my latte. Only eight hours before I'd be on my way back to my bed.

"You look really tired," Shayla said when she pulled up next to me in her bright yellow Volkswagen Beetle—the emoji on wheels.

"I am really tired," I replied with a laugh.

"That can only mean one thing." Her voice raised an octave.

"It wasn't nearly as good as you'd think."

We gathered our bags from the trunks of our cars and pulled on our gear belts that held a flashlight, pepper spray, a set of keys, and some gloves.

"Go on, tell me everything." Shayla's eyes sparkled in the late morning sun.

"Why are you so cheery? Is your mom out of town this week?" When her mom—the retired hard-assed cop—was out of town Shayla got full reign of the house and the freedom to be her sweet, unassuming self without criticism.

"Yes, but that's not—we're talking about you."

"Did you have a date?" I asked, narrowing my eyes at her.

She giggled and looked at the ground.

"And you weren't going to tell me about it?"

"It's early. I can't . . ."

I shook my head. "Oh come on." I protested, but no matter how much I prodded she wouldn't give up any details.

"I really want to hear about your night though," she said.

I almost objected since she wasn't dishing but didn't want to ruin her mood. "Well, he was completely drunk the entire night."

"Ugh. Say no more." She looked at herself in the tinted windows of her car, adjusting her hair into a bun that fit out the back of her ball cap. "You don't need that in your life."

I hesitated. "Well . . ."

"Well what?" She turned to face me with a what-have-you-done look on her face.

"I may have agreed to another date with him."

"Rylie." She shook her head. "Why do you insist on dating men who aren't good enough for you?"

"He apologized at the end of the night. It seemed pretty sincere." I could still feel the warmth of his hand on mine.

"What am I going to do with you?"

"I don't know, maybe tell me what you're hiding." I nudged her arm.

"I think we should probably get down to the plaza and help the opening rangers."

I turned on my radio. "Rangers Fourteen and Fifteen in service."

"Copy." Antonio's voice sent tingles down my spine. "Could you both come down to the plaza please?"

"Will do."

I turned to see Shayla standing with her hands on her hips.

"What?"

"You really shouldn't smile every time you hear his voice. He's one of the men I'm talking about."

"I don't smile every time. Plus he's married."

"I'm sure he's told you by now that his wife moved out," she said as we walked towards the shop and the summie trucks.

"He said something about them being separated. Do you know what happened?" I hated myself for asking the question.

"Nope. But I wouldn't count on it lasting forever. I've heard they've broken up like this before and always somehow end up back together."

"I hope they do work things out. For their sake," I said. "And anyway, I'm dating Garrett now."

"The drunk." Shayla frowned. "I'm starting to regret setting you up on Tinder."

"I'll be fine." I slid into my truck and turned over the ignition.

The plaza was packed. Families huddled under trees enjoying their freshly grilled meats that sent tendrils of flavor to my nose making my mouth water. Teenagers maneuvered paddleboards and pedal boats, splashing and giggling. Toddlers played in the sand on the swim beach while their mothers kept a watchful eye. The sight made my heart happy.

"It's about time you got down here," Antonio said from behind me.

I whipped around so quickly I almost lost my balance. "Why? It looks like all is well."

"Except for your little fan club." He pointed to where a group of twenty-somethings stood staring at me. "They have been here all morning waiting to meet you."

"YouTube," I rubbed the bridge of my nose. I had almost forgotten about the video.

"YouTube?" Shayla asked. "What do you mean YouTube?"

"Our very own Rylie Cooper and her snake bite are the newest YouTube sensation." He laid a giant hand on my shoulder and squeezed.

"What? How?" Shayla looked between the crowd

and me.

"There's a video of me being bested by that snake on the beach, and it went viral. The hostess last night even asked for my autograph."

Shayla covered her mouth with her hand trying to force her giggles from escaping.

"How did that date go?" Antonio's hand dropped from my shoulder leaving it lighter and lonely.

"It went great," I said, not meeting Shayla's eyes.

"Great, huh? So you'll be having another?"

"Yes. In fact, we're going to the Broncos game this weekend."

He let out a low whistle. "Sounds like he's smitten."

I ignored his raised eyebrow.

"Did I hear right that you found a body the other day?" Antonio continued.

"Yeah, over at Golden Rock Pond."

"Looks like you're a bit of a shit magnet. Two bodies in as many months after nothing for years." He took a step away and crossed his bulking arms over his chest. "Maybe I should request opposite shifts."

"There's no such thing as a shit magnet." I rolled my eyes. "Have you seen Seamus? Is he doing okay?"

"He's fine. He's still got his lucky charms and all." Antonio frowned.

The reservoir rangers and the trail rangers had a love-hate relationship.

"I'm sorry to hear about your separation," Shayla said.

I shifted from one foot to the other. Why would she bring it up now?

"It's been over longer than I wanted to admit. The fact

that I helped put her best friend's husband in prison was just the icing on the cake."

He glanced at me. It wasn't just his wife's best friend's husband. It was one of the former rangers and Antonio's best friends. And in the process, he had saved my life.

"Now I have to make sure she doesn't leave me high and dry." He stood a little taller. "I guess it's like the old saying. Love is like a fart. If you have to force it, it's probably shit. And we've been forcing it for far too long."

Shayla's hands flew up to cover her giggles. I almost let out a snort. "I've never heard that saying before."

He shrugged. "Maybe I made it up. But regardless, it's true."

That it was. I'd had my fair share of forcing love. And it had turned to shit pretty quickly.

We all stood in silence staring out at the beach. Tiny waves washed up on shore, nothing like what you'd see on the coast, but enough to make the kids squeal with delight. The lifeguards ran drills with a surprisingly life-like dummy. One of them would toss it into the water, and another would dive in to find it.

"You should probably get to talking to your fan club." Shayla motioned to the group of people patiently awaiting my attention. "Sign some autographs while I Google your video."

"It's hilarious," Antonio said. "I've watched it several times."

Of course he had.

I took a breath, plastered on a smile, and walked over to the eager crowd. My fifteen minutes could be up any time now.

7

After signing what felt like a hundred autographs and doing an impromptu speech on the difference between bullsnakes and rattlesnakes, I decided to take a loop around the reservoir to check some licenses and take a breather.

Fishermen that hadn't had a license check in the last hour covered the dam, and I needed the exercise. I walked up and down the worn and crumbling concrete stairs talking to every man, woman, and child. The fishing was no good—par for the hottest part of an early fall day—but the spirits were high. Several fishermen offered snacks, a chair, and not one mentioned my YouTube video or my Tinder presence. Score one for me.

When I reached the curve in the dam, I noticed a fisherman paying more attention to me than his line. "How's it going today?" I asked.

The man wearing khaki shorts and a bright white polo looked up from beneath the brim of his tan fishing hat.

Garrett. And lying on the concrete next to him was none other than his trusty sidekick, Babbitt.

"Hi Rylie," his deep voice bashful. "I-I probably shouldn't have come, but I just couldn't wait until Sunday to see you."

I could feel the goofy grin spread across my face as I reached down to pat Babbitt on the head.

"No boat today?" I rocked back on my heels tucking my hands into my pockets.

The fishing gear around him was as pristine as his home. A different tackle box than the one from the boat was open with neat rows of brightly colored lures and brand new jars of power bait. Notably absent were the prescription drug bottles. Had Seamus said something to him?

"Nah, I only had an hour or so. I'm just glad I caught you." He stood from his foldable camp chair and even though he stood two steps down from me, he still met my eye.

"I'm going to have to check your fishing license, you know." I held out a hand.

He bent down and fumbled around in the tackle box. "Here it is." He pulled it out triumphantly. "I had to get a replacement this morning. Couldn't find the other one."

It had probably blown out from the bottom of his boat where he'd tossed it after Seamus had checked it.

"Looks good." I handed it back to him.

"So are we still on for the game this weekend?" He looked down at his bright white ankle socks and Birkenstocks. "I understand if you've changed your mind after how poorly I acted last night."

"We're still on," I said, and he looked back up.

"Perfect. I'll pick you up—"

"That's okay." Panic welled in my chest. "I can meet you there." The last thing I needed him to know was that I lived in my parents' basement. He'd likely think I was only dating him for his money.

"Okay." He eyed me quizzically but didn't push. "Then I'll meet you in front of the stadium by the waterfall with the horses."

I'd never actually been to the stadium, but I figured I'd be able to find it. "Sounds great."

He stepped up to the step right in front of me and reached a hand up. "May I?"

I nodded and felt his fingers tuck a piece of stray hair behind my ear. His touch was gentle, his fingertips barely brushing the tip of my ear.

"There." He smiled and looked down into my eyes, his face dangerously close to mine.

He was going to kiss me. My heart nearly stopped.

He hooked a finger under my chin and kissed me gently on the cheek. "Thanks for giving me a second chance," he whispered in my ear then stepped back putting some space between us to combat the sparks.

I couldn't find my voice. My hand moved on its own up to my cheek. "You're welcome." I finally croaked out.

Garrett stood smiling at me as if we were the only two people on the dam . . . the dam. Dammit. I was working.

My heart began to beat again. What if someone saw him kiss me? One of the fishermen or Shayla or . . . Antonio?

I glanced around as subtly as I could, but no one seemed to be watching. I let out a breath.

"I should probably get back . . ."

"Of course." He smiled.

"See you Sunday."

"Can't wait."

I could feel his gaze on me while I walked the length of the dam back to my truck. Once safely within, I let out a short squeal.

"He kissed you?" Shayla asked when we sat down for a frozen TV dinner together at the shop.

"On the cheek." Heat rose to where the brush of his lips still lingered on my skin.

"You're lucky Antonio didn't see. He'd have probably punched the guy." Shayla pulled the plastic back on what looked like a frozen pile of mud claiming to be Salisbury steak and threw it in the microwave.

"Antonio needs to chill out. He's only been separated from his wife for what? A day?" I took a bite of my macaroni and cheese meal not sure whether that bite would still be cold as a polar bear's butt or hot as gooey yellow lava. There didn't seem to be much in between.

"Have you heard anything about that dead guy over on Golden Rock Trail?" Shayla asked.

"Nope. Luke's not exactly talking to me. Plus, I'm keeping my nose out of it, remember." I stuck out my tongue.

She rolled her eyes. "Do you think Boy Boy's out there lurking around, waiting to kill again?"

"Nah. He's probably holed up in someone's basement trying to stay away from the cops. Or in another state altogether." I took another bite. "The most logical thing is that he got his revenge on whoever this guy was and then high-tailed it to Canada."

"You're probably right. I just hate thinking he's out there."

"He's not the only murderer in the world. We have to be careful regardless."

Shayla pulled the muddy blob that smelled like canned dog food out of the microwave and took a bite, her face curling up in disgust. "I guess you're right." She looked up at the clock. "We should probably start closing up."

The plaza wasn't a welcoming place in the dark. The thatched tiki-style roofs threw creepy shadows across the concrete pathways in the moonlight. I pulled my jacket tighter around me.

Shayla chose the task of closing the walk-in gates while I locked up the plaza buildings. The plaza was the simpler of the two, but neither of us liked doing it.

After locking up the bathrooms, I began the long walk to the offices to set the alarms. Every sound made me jump. Being a park—even one within the city limits— meant critters, which meant noises.

But no critter sounded like heavy boots on concrete. I

turned and shined my flashlight in the eyes of the man sneaking up behind me.

"Whoa," he threw one hand over his eyes.

My chest constricted as I reached for my pepper spray. "Can I help you, sir?" I asked in the bravest voice I could muster.

"Rylie, it's me." The man's voice was familiar, but I had a hard time placing it. It probably didn't help that my heart was pounding in my ears.

I moved the flashlight beam down a hair, and he dropped his hand.

"Garrett?" I asked. "What are you doing here? I'm closing up the reservoir."

The look on his face was that of relief. Bags that hadn't been there that afternoon were now firmly planted under his eyes.

"Is everything okay?" I asked.

"Everything is great," he replied.

"Okay . . ."

"I'm sorry I scared you." He smiled at me. "Can I ask you for a favor?"

"Why didn't you ask me for this favor when I saw you this afternoon?" I looked down at my watch. I needed to get the rest of the plaza closed and the cars cleared from the park.

"Oh, well," he fidgeted with the keys in his hand, "This kinda came up last minute."

"Okay, sure. What do you need?" He quirked up one side of his mouth in a half smile that made my toes tingle.

"I have a package for my mom's birthday and I was

wondering if I could keep it in the trunk of your car. She's going to be visiting soon, and she tends to be a snoop."

Oh, how I knew about snoopy mothers. My own was probably going through my things as we spoke.

"No problem." I nodded. "Let me finish closing up this building, and I'll swing over and pick it up."

"Perfect," he let out a breath. Had he thought I'd turn him down? "I'm parked in that parking lot." He pointed to the main parking area for the beach.

"I'll be up in a bit," I said and turned to walk away.

"Thanks, Rylie," he called after me.

I turned and flashed him a smile. "Of course."

8

A fter setting the alarms on the office buildings, I practically ran back to my truck to meet Garrett and start clearing the parking lots. Shayla and I had to make sure there were no cars left in the park before we closed the gates because cars usually meant people and trapping people in the park overnight made them super mad.

I drove up to the main lot first to find Garrett's truck sitting in the middle of the lot plus a small silver car parked in one of the corners, almost hidden from view. I'd have to track down the owner after I got done with Garrett.

"I'll just throw the box into the truck and put it in the back of my car once I get back to the shop," I said to Garrett when I opened the passenger door.

He pulled a brown shipping box big enough to hold my huge gear bag plus my uniform and duty belt from his messy cab and transferred it to the ranger truck, slamming the door behind it.

"What'd you get her?" I asked as he picked up the empty soda bottles that had fallen onto the asphalt when he'd opened the door of his truck.

Garrett looked as if I'd been speaking another language but he rubbed his eyes and snapped out of it. "Uh, it's a quilt I had made for her out of my childhood clothes."

"That's so sweet. How long do you want me to keep it?"

"Only a week or so."

I looked up into his eyes. I knew I needed to finish closing up, but my feet seemed cemented to the ground. "No problem."

In one fluid motion, he crooked an arm behind my back and lifted me completely off the ground, planting his lips on mine.

Where there had been sparks before, now there were fireworks. I lost all track of time and place. The only thing that mattered was that kiss.

It was over as quickly and abruptly as it had begun. He gently reunited my feet with the ground and gave me a cocky smile. "Thanks again."

"You're welcome. I'll see you on Sunday."

"Sunday." He made finger guns at me as he walked back to his truck. "See you then."

Once he had gone, I only had to check on the owner of the silver car. I parked next to it, pulling my flashlight from my belt.

"Anyone in there?" I shined the light inside the car and tapped on the window. No response. "Perfect." I searched the dark plaza area and shoreline. I needed to find this person and quickly. It was well past closing time.

"Ranger Fourteen, Ranger Fifteen," I called out on the radio.

"Fifteen, go ahead," Shayla's voice came back through my mic.

"I have one car left up here. I'm going to be on foot looking for the owner."

"Copy. I'm headed back to get the gates. I had some fishermen who forgot we close at dark." The sound of her voice gave away how much she believed their forgetfulness.

"Did you issue a citation?" I asked knowing full well she hadn't. Neither of us had written our first tickets.

"No. Only a warning." She replied.

"Copy. Clear."

I locked the truck and began the walk down the steps to the plaza. I was too pissed to be afraid anymore. I was over this shift. The only thing keeping me half-way sane was the memory of the spine-numbing kiss I'd just had.

"Anyone down here? The park is closing." I shined my flashlight down the shoreline just as I heard an engine rev from behind me in the parking lot.

The silver car's engine hummed, it's lights flashed on, and it tore out of the parking lot.

In the dark, I couldn't make out the license plate number. Now if they came back and were late again, I'd couldn't issue them a citation. Dammit.

I made my way back to the ranger truck, cleared the rest of the lots, and went to park entrance to close up.

"Ranger Fourteen, Ranger Fifteen," I called out on the radio after closing the main gate.

Shayla didn't answer.

"Ranger Fourteen, Ranger Fifteen," I called again. Why wasn't she answering? She always responded on the first call.

What if Boy Boy or . . .

No.

I'm sure there was a perfectly reasonable explanation. Deep breaths in and out.

She had her radio turned down or she was talking to someone and lost track of time. Or maybe she had decided to issue a citation after all.

"Ranger Fourteen, Ranger Fifteen. Status?" I asked.

Come on. Respond.

I turned the truck around and headed down the path to the back gates.

"Ranger Fifteen." Her voice was quiet. Distant.

"What is your status?" I said into the radio.

"I'm by gate three," her small voice came back. "I need . . . help."

I floored it. "Are you hurt? Do I need to call an ambulance?"

"It—it's too late—" her mic cut out.

I'd never driven so fast on the path but knowing there weren't any bikers or joggers made it more like a NASCAR road course than a bike path. Regardless of my speed, it seemed to take forever to get to Shayla. I rounded the last corner and spotted Shayla's truck right next to gate three.

My truck had barely come to a stop when I threw it in park and jumped out.

"Shayla?" I called out.

"Over here," I heard her squeak from the tall grass next to the gate.

I ran, pepper spray in hand. But when Shayla's blonde ringlets came into view, I knew I didn't need to protect myself.

Shayla crouched in front of what appeared to be a partially decomposed body, sans head. I put a hand on Shayla's shoulder, and she turned to look up at me. Tears streaked down her face.

"Come on, let's call Luke," I said.

9

Luke arrived within a matter of minutes. He wrapped Shayla up in a big hug as I stood to the side watching his partner Jerry take photos of the body and the crime scene.

"What is it with you and finding dead bodies?" Jerry said in his toad-like voice.

"I didn't find it. Shayla did."

"Still. You was here." He picked up a black hair ribbon and placed it in a Ziploc evidence bag. "Looks like you're a shit magnet."

I'd give my left arm for everyone to stop calling me that.

"This lady was having a bad day," Jerry said. "How'd you find her?"

Shayla glanced up from Luke's chest, and I tried to tamp down the utterly unwarranted twinge of jealousy. "I thought I heard something so I walked over and—"

The rest of her sentence was cut off by her heaving up the regurgitated mud-like Salisbury steak all over Luke's chest. It looked and smelled about the same as it had before she ate it.

Luke patted her on the head, his gaze averted.

"Uh, you should probably clean yourself up," I said to Luke as I rubbed Shayla's back. "I'll take care of her."

Every cop I knew had a weak stomach. Let the firefighter—ex-firefighter—handle the job.

"It's okay. Get it all out," I said.

Shayla wretched again.

"That's disgusting," Jerry yelled. "You're screwing up the crime scene."

I gently pulled Shayla away while glaring at Jerry. "It's okay, don't listen to him."

"It was a cat," Shayla said between sobs. "The noise. It was a cat. Meowing and . . . eating." she gagged.

"Yuck. Don't finish that sentence," I said.

"I'm sorry I didn't call you or answer quickly." She stood from her hunched position. "I saw her and I—I froze. Some police officer I'll be."

"It's your first dead body, and a gross one at that." I glanced over to where the body still lay, taking a closer look. It had been a woman around five foot with sky-high red stilettos and a pink mini skirt. The severed neck was disgusting enough but seeing a cat eating it would turn anyone's stomach.

"She's been here a while. Probably a week or so." Jerry walked over to us.

Luke had removed his soiled shirt and stood at the

trunk of his car bare-chested. His muscles were more prominent than they had been in high school. His abs looked like they'd been chiseled by a sculptor. I looked away but not quickly enough. Luke had already caught me staring.

"You all right, Shay?" he asked.

"Better." She nodded. The color in her cheeks hadn't returned, but at least she wasn't throwing up anymore. "Do you think—was it Boy Boy?"

"No way to know at this point," Jerry said. "Heck, we don't even know for sure the last one was Boy Boy's vic. Might've just been a coinkidink."

"We might be here a while." Luke pulled on a Prairie City PD hoodie. "You should probably call a supervisor."

Duh. Why hadn't I thought of that?

"Antonio lives the closest," Shayla said without meeting my eye.

"Can you call him?" I asked.

"I think I'm going to be sick again." She gave me a sly smile. "You better do it."

It was my turn to feel nauseous.

"I'm glad you called me," Antonio said when he arrived. He drove his black CTS-V—a total contrast from the sweatpants and Denver Broncos hoodie he wore.

"It was Shayla's idea," I mumbled. I'd kept the phone call short and sweet—another dead body . . . I know, shit magnet . . . Need a supervisor . . . Bye.

"Luke, it's nice to see you again." He held out a hand, which Luke grasped and shook twice.

"So what's going on?"

"Dead body. Decapitated," Jerry said. "The snake wrangler over there found it."

Shit magnet and snake wrangler. I was getting quite a name for myself. And not one that was going to help me get the full-time job.

Luke and Antonio both burst out laughing.

"I don't know what the big deal is," I said crossing my arms over my chest.

"It's not every day people get to see a hot park ranger get bested by a harmless little snake," Luke said.

"He wasn't so harmless." I rubbed my thumb over the nearly non-existent bite marks, trying not to think too much about Luke calling me hot. "And definitely not little."

"She has a point, that snake was huge," Antonio said.

"Eh, I've seen bigger," Shayla said in a small voice.

Everyone stopped and stared at her before we all doubled over in laughter. I couldn't believe sweet Shayla would say such a thing.

"Hey, we got a dead body over here," Jerry shouted over our laughter. "Show some respect."

His tone was non-negotiable.

We stopped laughing.

"I hear you had a date the other night," Luke said.

"Where'd you hear that?" I asked. Was he going to come clean that he'd seen me?

"I hear everything."

"She met him on Tinder," Antonio chimed in. They both stood in front of me with their hands on their hips.

"So what if I did?" I mirrored their stances. "He's a great guy."

"He's taking her to the Broncos game this weekend," Antonio said.

"And he kissed her today," Shayla added.

"Shayla!" I shot her a sideways glare.

"What? I thought we were sharing what we knew." She shrugged. "Maybe I'm still in shock?"

Uh-huh, shock.

"Wow, first kiss, huh?" Luke said.

"How's Nikki?" I blurted out.

"She's fine." He looked down at his shoes that still had bits of regurgitated Salisbury steak on them.

"Ah that's right, you're Nikki's new flame," Antonio said. Antonio and Nikki went way back, but I didn't detect much jealousy in his voice.

"Did she say something about me?" Luke asked.

"Just that she's a bit irritated with you." Antonio seemed to be enjoying this way too much.

"Why's she mad?" I asked nonchalantly.

"I'm going out of town the next couple of days. Down to Winslow, Arizona—"

"Are you going to stand on a corner?" Shayla asked.

Luke grinned at her. "No, I have to talk to the police down there about Boy Boy's escape."

"So she's mad that you're going out of town?" I asked, trying to bring the subject back around to him and Nikki.

"That and we had a crappy date the other night," Luke said quickly.

76

A crappy date?

"You couldn't stop staring at some other girl," Antonio said wiggling his eyebrows at Luke.

Luke's face paled.

I turned to Shayla, "I think it's time we head home."

Shayla looked up from her pants, now covered in vomit and dirt. "Good idea."

T hursday morning I woke up early to run still in a state of disbelieve that we'd found two dead bodies in a matter of four days. I drove to Alder Ridge Reservoir and parked outside of gate three. Was I secretly hoping Luke was still there? Maybe.

But he wasn't. In fact, no one was. Oh well.

I tucked in my earbuds and blared old Brittney Spears music.

My pace and overall fitness had drastically improved over the course of the summer. The vacant full-time position drove me to work harder and more diligently. If I didn't get the job, I'd probably wind up overweight and unemployed.

A complete loop around the reservoir was fifteen miles, but I hadn't quite built the stamina to go that far so when I reached Muddy Water Cove, I turned and ran back towards gate three.

The higher the sun rose, the more sweat accumulated

on my brow. It may have been fall but the weather hadn't gotten the memo.

The trees stood lifeless in the still air. Their leaves just waiting for a cold snap to turn copper and fall.

As I rounded the last corner, I saw a tiny black box mounted with a black strap the width of a man's belt to one of the tree trunks. It could have easily been missed, especially driving in a truck.

I slowly approached and inspected it. It looked like a camera of some sort.

I had to let the ranger on duty know. I punched the number of the park office into my cell.

"Alder Ridge Reservoir, this is Carmen," a bubbly voice that matched its owner in every way said.

"Hey Carmen, it's Rylie. Who's working this morning?"

"Ben and Greg," she replied. "They just got back from their big bow hunting trip. They were saying they got two big bucks and—"

"Carmen?"

"Yeah, sorry. What did you need?"

"Can you send them back to gate three? I need to show them something."

"For the love of God tell me you didn't find another dead body."

I sighed. "No."

"That's good 'cause they've been calling you the shit—"

"I know what they've been calling me." I steadied my voice. "Can you please just ask them to come back here when they get a chance? Please?"

"Sure thing sweetheart." Her voice lowered to a whisper. "Did I tell you I stopped seeing Dave?"

"No." Dave was her disgusting lover with whom she cheated on her wealthy husband.

"It's for the best."

"I'm sorry."

"It's okay." Her voice came back to full strength. "I'll get them to head back as soon as they can."

"Perfect. Thanks," I said, but she didn't hear me because she had already started greeting a guest.

"Hi there," she said before she slammed the receiver down, disconnecting the call.

I inspected the little box again. Who would want to film this trail? Probably some pervert who got off on women jogging. I wrapped my arms around my chest suddenly feeling like I needed a shower.

Nearly thirty minutes later a ranger truck came around the corner. I was sitting on the side of the path on a log checking my Tinder results. Sure, I had a date with Garrett, but that didn't mean I was off the market.

"It took you long enough," I said when Ben stepped out of the truck. Ben looked like a mixture of the Rock and the Hulk with only a tiny bit more hair than the Rock.

"I think Carmen forgot. She only told me five minutes ago."

"I heard your bow hunting trip went well."

"Yep." He smiled. "Now onto rifle season."

Most of the rangers hunted. That's why they kept the summies on the schedule into the fall.

"What'd you find?"

I pointed in the direction of the little box on the tree. "I don't know what it is. It kinda looks like a camera. Probably some perv trying to get pictures of women running."

"That?" He let out a belly laugh. "I'll let Seamus know you think he's a perv."

"Seamus?" Now I was thoroughly confused.

"He got a grant for these cameras about a month ago. They're supposed to capture photos of wildlife habits and park violations."

Of course. Trail cams. "Okay. Sorry about calling you out here for this."

"It's no big deal. Nothing is going on now that the dead bodies have been carted away." He nudged my shoulder with his arm. "You know, if I didn't know any better I'd say you were—"

"If you call me a shit magnet, I'll have another dead body on my hands."

He put his hands up in surrender. "Whoa, sorry." He laughed. "Is snake wrangler any better?"

I lunged at him, and he ran back to his truck laughing. "I won't forget to tell Seamus you think he's a perv." He yelled out his window as he drove past me.

Trail cameras. "Wait!" I waved my hands to get Ben's attention. The brake lights lit up, and the truck came to an abrupt halt.

I ran to his window.

"You're not going to attack me are you?" He laughed again.

"Are the trail cameras always on?"

"Yeah. They're motion activated. It keeps the batteries

from wearing out as quickly, and Seamus is pretty good about changing them out when they're low."

"Is Seamus working this morning?"

"He's out by Area Twelve. Why?"

"I need to talk to him."

It took Seamus and Brock forty-five minutes to make it to the shop where they met Ben and me in the office.

"This had better be good. We were taking down a homeless camp," Brock said as he walked in after Seamus.

I ignored him. "Seamus, I found one of your trail cams."

"They're not exactly hidden, Blondie."

"I know, I know." Come on Rylie get to the point. "Do you have a map of where they're all located?"

"Map's in me head."

"Are there any over by Golden Rock Pond?"

"Not really . . ."

"But there's the one here, by gate three."

"Yes."

"How often do you check it?"

"Every week or so." He tapped his foot on the ground. "Why? What's this all about?"

"Maybe they can tell us—or the police—who killed that lady."

Seamus slapped himself on the forehead. "Yer a genius. Why didn't I think of that?"

I shrugged and smiled from ear to ear.

"I'll go get the memory card now," Seamus said.

"Can I come with?" I asked.

"Isn't today your day off?" Brock asked, his arms crossed over his chest. "And what about the homeless camps?"

"We can get the card and bring them back here. The homeless camp will have to wait," he said to Brock who was pouting like a two-year-old.

"Better call that cop boyfriend of yers," Seamus said. "He'll want to see this."

"He's not my boyfriend," I said.

"That's right." A hiss from behind me knocked the smile right off my face. "He's *my* boyfriend."

We all spun around to find Nikki standing in the doorway. "What are you going on about anyway?"

"Rylie just had a brilliant idea," Ben said. His face was lit up like the Christmas tree he apparently kept up in his house year-round.

"She did, did she?" Nikki looked down at her pretty pink nails. "And what's that?"

"She thinks there might be pictures of the murderer or murderers on the trail cam by gate three," Seamus said. "It's bloody brilliant."

"Or common sense," Nikki said.

Common sense? She hadn't thought of it.

"We need to get these murders solved. I have my first event coming up this weekend, and I don't want it spoiled with news of a murderer leaving dead bodies all over my parks."

Her parks? And, sure, we'd get right on solving these murders so her little event wouldn't be affected.

Nikki had gotten the full-time job that included

managing events to promote visitor growth and produce income for the parks. I'd interviewed for the job but couldn't quite figure out the correct way to get out of a blender.

"I'll get the memory card and meet yeh back here in a little bit. Is Shayla closing tonight?" Seamus ran a hand through his hair.

"Yep. In fact, I'm supposed to meet her in about five minutes to work out before her shift." My stomach grumbled. I hadn't had a chance to go home since my morning run. I stunk and was starving. "I'll see you later."

"Don't forget to call yer boy—" he looked at Nikki's glare, "Er, friend, and let him know."

fter grabbing a protein bar and applying an extra coating of deodorant to my armpits, I texted Luke.

You free this afternoon to come out to the reservoir?

Yeah, Nikki told me about the trail cam footage.

Of course she had.

K.

I shoved the phone into my work bag and headed up to the loft where Shayla waited for me.

"I hear you made a break in the case," she said. Her long blonde hair was curled and in a ponytail and she'd lined her eyes with a perfect cat eye. If only I didn't sweat so much when I worked out, I'd be able to look cute too.

"Not exactly." I wrapped my hands in boxing tape. "Not yet anyway. We'll see what the camera shows."

"I really hope we can figure out who's been doing all of this. That girl probably has a family somewhere worried sick about her." Her eyes welled with tears. Hopefully, she'd gone with waterproof eyeliner.

"I hope so too. And maybe if it is Boy Boy, we can get a feel for his movements so we can catch him."

"*We*? No. *We* are not going to catch him. *We* are going to let Luke and Jerry catch him. Right?" She stared at me.

"That's what I meant. Geeze." I gave her a whoa-buddy look.

"I don't want to see you get hurt." She turned the treadmill on.

"It'll be fine. I won't get in the middle of it. I promise." How many times did I have to promise to stay out of it? It was as if they thought I *liked* being in the middle of these investigations.

"I can't believe our season is almost over. Are you still going to apply for the full-time position?"

"If they ever post it. What about you?" I hated the thought of having to go against Shayla.

"Nah. I want you to get it. I'm really hoping I get accepted to the fall police academy."

"Brock said he's applying to the academy too." I hit the punching bag hard feeling the shock waves move through the tension in my back.

"Wouldn't it be funny if we were in the same class?"

"I'd go with annoying or dangerous over funny," I said spinning around and kicking the bag. "I still don't think he should be given a gun."

Shayla laughed. "He's exactly like so many of the guys Mom used to work with. Minus Luke, of course."

Luke. I hesitated mid-kick, my leg barely making contact with the bag.

"Sorry, let's not talk about Luke." Shayla turned the speed up. "Why don't you tell me more about Garrett?"

Garrett. I'd almost forgotten about him between the dead bodies and Luke and Antonio and Tinder. "I forgot to tell you in the commotion, but he came back to the reservoir to ask a favor last night."

She wiggled her eyebrows at me. "Ooh, a favor."

"Not that kind of favor. He needed me to hold onto his mother's birthday gift. He did kiss me though."

"Like a real kiss?" She asked and tripped nearly falling off the end of the treadmill.

"Be careful," I said. "And yes, like a real holy crap kiss. I didn't know he had it in him. It may have been one of the best kisses I've ever had."

"Presents for his mom, Broncos tickets, *and* a good kisser. It's a trifecta of awesomeness. If only he wasn't a heavy drinker."

"He was nervous. He said he wouldn't drink at the game." The more I thought about it, the more he seemed like the type of guy I was looking for. As long as he kept his promise.

"Is he picking you up on Sunday?"

"No. I don't really want him to know I live with my parents." Hopefully, I'd get the full-time job and a place of my own before he needed to know where I lived. That is if the date went well.

"Any other hits on Tinder?" she asked.

"Not really." The leather of the bag was becoming more malleable from the heat of my rapid punches. "There are a lot of sleazeballs out there."

"Tell me about it."

"That reminds me. Are you going to tell me about your date the other day?"

Shayla's perfectly primped face turned pink. "I—I mean I would but—"

"You guys up there?" Luke's voice came from the shop below. I stopped hitting the bag.

"Yep. Come on up," Shayla said. I made a mental note to ask her about the date again.

Luke appeared on the spiral staircase looking like he'd just walked off the cover of *Preppy-Prep Magazine*.

"Whoa, were you having tea with the Queen?" I teased.

He glanced down at his blue polo and khakis complete with sweater draped over his shoulders and tied at the neck. "Can't a guy look nice?"

"She has a point." Shayla stepped off the treadmill completely sweat free. "You do look like you were at the —" Shayla's eyes widened. "You were at the country club with Nikki weren't you?"

Luke looked down at his brown loafers. "She wanted me to meet her family."

I silently prayed my mother would never know he was spending time with another woman's family. It would break her heart.

"And?" Shayla pried.

"And what?" He gave her a disinterested look. He and

Shayla had more of a brother-sister relationship than Shayla wanted to admit. "It was fine, okay?"

"Fine?" I chimed in. "Fine isn't good."

"They're . . . different. Not in a bad way," he added quickly. "I have to step my game up with them."

I steadied my face. I couldn't let him see how much it hurt that he was making such an effort to impress Nikki's family.

"Are we going to look at the pictures or not?" His patience had run out.

"Seamus isn't here yet," Shayla said not looking up at Luke.

"Did someone say my name?" Seamus's voice came from the stairs.

Shayla's head popped up, and she gave Seamus a huge smile.

Of course.

Why hadn't I seen it before? Seamus was the guy she was hiding. The smile he gave her in return confirmed my suspicions.

Definitely an item.

It took everything in me not to squeal and tell her I knew.

"Before we look at the photos, I wanted to give you an update on what we know about the deceased," Luke said.

"Perfect." Shayla tore her eyes from Seamus's, "Do you know the identity of the girl? Have you contacted her family?"

"We've notified both families. Apparently, the two of them were dating. We haven't figured out why they were killed separately, but they went missing on the same day," Luke said.

"Are they connected to Boy Boy?" I asked.

"Yes. At least, the man was. The woman was by association, but that's all we know about her right now. The autopsies haven't come back yet."

"Shall we go look at the photos?" Seamus seemed far too excited for what we might see on that memory card.

"Maybe I should look at them alone first," Luke said. "In case they contain sensitive material."

"I can handle it," I said.

"Are yeh kiddin'?" Seamus said. "I see terrible things all the time out there."

Luke looked at Shayla. "You don't have to be tough. I know how hard it was on you to see that woman's body."

"It was a bit of a shock." She took a step away from Luke and towards Seamus. "But I have to get used to seeing things like this if I want to become a police officer, right?"

Luke looked like he was going to object but instead gave a silent nod.

"All right, then. If we're all in agreement. Let's go see what we got." Seamus led us down the stairs and into the office where he plugged in the memory card.

Hundreds of tiny photo thumbnails popped up on the screen.

The camera at the reservoir was only about twenty feet from gate three and was aimed at the gate itself. There were hundreds of photos of walkers and bikers, dogs and deer and even a coyote.

The photos taken at night had an infrared look similar to the video games my ex-boyfriend, Troy, played for hours on end.

"We estimate the woman died about a week ago," Luke said.

Seamus scrolled to the photos on those dates. "Stop me if yeh see something I miss." He clicked through the pictures quickly. "Benny said yeh think I'm a creeper."

"I'm pretty sure the word I used was pervert," I replied. "But that was before I knew what you used these cameras for. Or that it was you who had the cameras."

"Pervert or creeper or whatever, they may have just—"

"Stop," Luke said. "Right there."

Sure enough, there was a photo of a large man dragging a woman's limp body—head attached—into the gate.

"That definitely looks like Boy Boy," Luke said. "Can you send me that picture so I can have the lab take a closer look?"

"Done." Seamus sent the email. "If she had her head when he went in . . ."

The next photo showed the man from behind holding a sports bag with brown hair fluttering out the unzipped top.

"You better send that one too," Luke said.

I felt Shayla sway next to me. I squeezed her hand. "You okay?"

Seamus looked over at her like he wanted to comfort her too, but he turned back to the computer screen.

Luke looked back and forth between them and quirked a questioning eyebrow up at me. I shrugged. I wasn't going to give away a secret I wasn't even supposed to be keeping.

"I guess the only thing left now is to find Boy Boy," Luke said.

12

Ben announced that Nikki was holding a pre-event meeting the moment I walked into the shop for my shift Friday afternoon.

"Do I have to be there?" I whined.

"Everyone does. Even those not scheduled to work the event."

I pulled on my button-down uniform shirt, tucked it in, and strapped on my duty belt. "That's ridiculous."

Ben shrugged. "It is what it is. No need to get our panties in a wad."

"I guess we should get down there then." I tossed my work bag into the summie truck. "Wouldn't want to make Princess Nikki wait."

Ben let out a hesitant laugh. I knew he liked Nikki, all the rangers did, but for the life of me, I couldn't figure out why. She was vile. Case in point: her tapping foot the moment I walked in the room.

"It's about time you showed up. We've been waiting for you," she hissed under her breath as I walked by.

I wanted to bite back that my shift had just started and if she wanted me there earlier she should have let me know, but I held my tongue. All of the rangers sat around a long set of tables with Ursula at the head.

The only seat open after Ben had taken a seat next to Greg was the one beside Antonio.

I sat and saw Antonio's smug smile and intense gaze out of the corner of my eye.

"Thank you all for coming here today," Nikki said in her honey-sweet voice taking her place next to Ursula. "We thought it would good for everyone to be here since it's our first triathlon."

Brock shifted in his seat. It was his day off, and he looked none too pleased that he had to be here for the meeting. Especially since he wasn't scheduled to work the event.

"Going forward, we'll only have these meetings for the staff scheduled for each individual event." She beamed at Ursula who gave an approving nod. "What I'm passing out now are the event details."

She sauntered around the table, not in uniform but in skinny jeans and a blush chiffon blouse that accentuated her long wavy red hair. She dropped one of the packets in front of me that was at least fifty pages long.

I thumbed through the pages finding maps, detailed job descriptions, and an intricate timeline including things like course marked, first swimmer in water, and water bottles to finish line. It was enough to make my head throb.

Antonio nudged me in the side, and I nearly let out a shriek.

"This is nuts," he whispered.

I nodded but kept my head down. If Ursula hadn't been present, I'd have joked along with him, but I needed her to think I was a good choice for that full-time position.

"Open your packets please."

The rustle of paper turning from the cover to page one fluttered through the room along with a few sighs.

"We'll begin on page one," Nikki said, her voice almost giddy with excitement. As much as I hated to admit it, she had been the right one for the job. I never could have made such goo-goo eyes at a piece of paper showing a topographical map with a race course marked in bright red. "As you can see the map of the reservoir shows the race course. The competitors will begin with the 750-meter swim, move onto the 20-kilometer bike section, then finish with a 5-kilometer run."

Just the thought of this competition made me tired. My sister had done her fair share of triathlons, even after having the boys. She'd once tried to get me to do one with her, but any thoughts of me competing had ceased when I tried to squish myself into her teeny-tiny wetsuit.

"Approximately five hundred competitors will enter the water from the swim beach in waves of one hundred."

"Excuse me?" Greg raised his hand but didn't wait for Nikki's approval to continue. "Are you saying you're going to fit a hundred people through the ten yard opening between the ranger dock and the swim line five times over?"

Nikki shifted in her seat. "Yes." She looked to Ursula who nodded for her to continue. "We're working very closely with the event organizers who assure us this is how they have run multiple events previously."

"Why aren't they here?" Brock asked.

"The event organizers are responsible only for their event. I am responsible for the rangers and organizing the staff."

She was our boss now?

It surprised me there wasn't even a single hint of reaction to her statement. Until I saw Ursula's face practically daring any of us to defy Nikki.

I restrained my urge to huff, cross my arms over my chest, and slouch in my seat. Instead, I smiled sweetly through gritted teeth.

"To continue"—Nikki sat up a bit straighter—"the swimmers will exit the water on the far side of the swim beach, run up to the parking lot while peeling off their wetsuits—"

Brock snickered.

"—and get to their bikes where they'll put on their shoes, shorts, and shirts before beginning the bike portion highlighted on page five."

Everyone turned to page five where the bike course was drawn in a bright yellow.

"They'll bike north out onto the roads away from the city. The event organizers hired several police officers, aid vehicles will be on standby, and we will not be dealing with any issues on the bike course."

I could feel my eyelids getting heavy. The thought of headless bicyclists floated through my mind, and it wasn't until Antonio nudged me with his foot that I realized I'd been in a serious daydream.

I searched the room, but no one seemed to be paying me any attention at all. In fact, Nikki was still droning on but was now halfway through the book and was talking enthusiastically about the race sponsors. Antonio nudged me again, and I turned and looked at his paper.

> *Wake up. You're not going to get the full-time position sleeping on the job.*

His writing was tiny and slanted to the right.

I pulled my pen from my uniform pocket and wrote on my own paper, trying to make it look like I was taking notes about the sponsors Nikki babbled on about.

> *I wasn't sleeping.*

He put his pen back to his paper, and I looked back up at Nikki. Ursula narrowed her eyes at me. Had she caught us writing notes?

Antonio nudged my foot again, but I didn't look. Ursula was still watching with her hawk-like stare. I glanced down at my packet, now open to the completely wrong page.

I felt a nudge in my ribs. Antonio wasn't letting up. I glanced to see if Ursula had diverted her attention to someone else. She hadn't.

I shook my head down at my page, trying to tell Antonio to leave it alone for a minute, but he didn't get the message. This time the nudge was harder and a squeak burst from my lips.

Every eye in the room turned to us. It felt like flames were engulfing my face.

"Is there something you need to tell Rylie, Antonio?" Ursula hissed.

Antonio let out a breath. "No, ma'am."

I didn't dare look up at anyone in the room for fear of breaking into laughter. It wasn't funny. Shouldn't be funny. It was my potential future on the line, but the thought of Shayla's giggle or Ben's snicker was almost enough to set off my own funny bone.

"Are you absolutely sure?" Ursula asked.

I willed her silently to let it go.

"Because it looked as if you were trying to get her attention pretty desperately." Ursula was on her feet and standing behind us now. "May I?" She picked up the piece of paper Antonio had been writing on and then snatched my own before I could close it.

The air in the room was stiflingly still as if no one even dared breathe.

"It seems as though this entire meeting has become a laughing matter to these two." Ursula threw the two packets back in front of us, and I caught what looked like an invitation to dinner written on Antonio's packet under his first note, but before I could read it all the way, he picked the paper up and turned back to the first page. "Let's take a break."

We all stood and hurried out of the room.

"What were you writing notes about?" Shayla asked when we walked outside into the warm sun and fresh air.

"Antonio was only telling me not to fall asleep."

Shayla shook her head. "That felt like being in middle school all over again. How much of all of that did you take in?"

"I think I stopped listening when Nikki started her inch by inch description of the race course." I looked around to make sure Nikki and Ursula were out of earshot. "Why is it so important we know all of this?"

"It's Nikki's way of making herself feel important," Brock said from behind me. "It's complete bullshit that I had to be here."

I couldn't argue with him on that one.

"PCPD dispatch to any ranger on duty at Alder Ridge Reservoir," a woman's voice said over the radios.

Several of us reached for our mics before Greg waved a hand indicating he would take it.

"This is Ranger One, go ahead dispatch."

"We've just gotten a report of a man running on the backside of the reservoir nude."

Naked guy strikes again.

"Copy. We'll check it out," Greg replied.

"Thank you. Dispatch clear."

"Who wants it?" Greg asked the group.

All of our hands shot up like a bunch of school kids. Anything to get us out of listening to more of Nikki's presentation.

"Not Rylie," Ursula's said from behind me. "I need to speak with her."

A chill ran down my spine. I felt like I was being called to the principal's office.

"Dusty should go since he won't be at the event,"

Nikki said. Greg nodded, and Dusty was gone before anyone could contradict the choice. Lucky.

"The rest of you have five more minutes before we reconvene," Nikki said and then marched back into the building her kitten heels tapping on the cement.

I turned to find Ursula standing much too close for comfort. Though I towered over her, her stare made me feel about an inch tall.

"Follow me," she said, then marched away from the group gaping at us.

I followed until she stopped dead in her tracks under a large aspen tree.

"Do you know why I want to speak with you?" she asked, her arms crossed over her chest wrinkling her tailored pantsuit.

"Because Antonio and I were writing notes?" I put my hands in my pockets so my fidgeting wouldn't give away my nervousness.

"Because you made a fool of yourself and a fool of this reservoir and a fool of the entire city."

"By writing that I wasn't falling asleep?" I tried to keep my voice as professional as possible, but this lady was making a huge deal out of such a small thing.

"Not by writing notes. By being in that snake video."

Oh.

"I didn't know the video would go viral. I was trying to do my job and the snake and the sandcastle and—"

She held up her hand. I closed my mouth. Damn verbal vomit.

"We paid you for an entire week of snake handling training, and you still couldn't get it right."

"I know. I didn't realize how much harder it would be in real life." Tears stung at my eyes. I would not cry. "Next time I'll do better."

"I certainly hope during your *last* month of employment there will not be another encounter with a snake. And if there is, it better not be in front of a camera."

Did she think I wanted to be filmed making an ass of myself? That I wanted thousands of people to see an edited version of what happened so they could laugh at my expense?

"Are you saying I shouldn't apply for the full-time position once it's posted?" I asked, my voice shaky and quiet.

"I'm saying one more misstep will be cause for immediate termination. As far as the full-time position, I can't tell you not to apply but—"

"Ranger Four, Ranger One?" Dusty's voice came from the mic on my shoulder.

"Go ahead," Greg replied.

"Naked man has been apprehended . . . again."

I heard snickers come from the group of rangers behind me.

"Copy. Thanks."

Even the thought of a naked man running through the park couldn't lift my spirits. All my hard work trying to prove myself over the summer was for naught.

"Let's go everyone," Nikki called from behind me.

Ursula shot one last glare in my direction and marched away towards the lifeguards on the swim beach mumbling something about them losing one of the expensive rescue dummies. I wiped the tears from my eyes, took a deep breath, and turned to follow Nikki back inside.

Shayla and Antonio stood with matching looks of worry on their faces as I approached. I shook my head and walked past taking my seat back at the table.

"What happened?" Antonio whispered when he sat down next to me.

I didn't dare look up from the papers in front of me for fear everyone would see my bloodshot eyes.

"Nothing," was all I could manage to say.

His hand twitched as if it would move to comfort me, but instead, he clenched it into a fist.

Nikki returned to her rambling event speech. I tried to listen, but what was the point? It didn't matter anymore whether I tried to be a good ranger. My days were numbered. I needed to find another job quickly, or else it would be goodbye car, goodbye freedom, and goodbye future.

"What did she say to you?" Shayla asked after Nikki had finished and the group had disbursed.

Antonio had tried to get my attention several more times during the meeting, but I didn't want to give Ursula a reason to terminate me, so I ignored him. Thankfully, Ben pulled him away when the meeting was over before he could question me.

"She said I embarrassed the city and I shouldn't even apply for the full-time position."

"What? How?"

"The snake video." A tear wandered its way down my chin. I swiped it away hopeful the guys hadn't seen it.

"She said I should have known how to handle it and if I made one more misstep she would fire me on the spot."

"Holy moly. That's terrible. I'm sorry." Shayla put her arm around me and squeezed. "You could always apply for police academy with Brock and me."

Police academy was an option, but my heart just wasn't in police work. Deep down I was more the fire-fighter type.

"I guess it's something to consider," I said.

"Are you going to be okay closing tonight?" she asked.

"Yeah. Ben's easy to get along with."

"If you need to talk, you can call me."

"Thanks." I gave her a smile and headed to my truck. I needed to get as far away from everyone as I could.

13

"**O**kay people. Today is the day. Don't screw this up." It was the butt crack of dawn on Saturday morning, and Nikki had us lined up like soldiers ready to do her bidding.

"I need all of you exactly where we discussed."

With everything that had gone on, I had failed to pay attention to my event assignment. That mixed with my searching for jobs until one in the morning left me with bags under my eyes too large for any concealer to touch.

I glanced to my right where Shayla stood with a look of exhaustion on her face. She had listened in the meeting. She'd be able to tell me what I was doing.

"Any questions? There shouldn't be."

I considered raising my hand but thought better of it. She'd likely chop it off.

"If you have an emergency, call me first."

Or an ambulance.

"Now go." Nikki turned and marched away to give the lifeguards their orders.

"Do you remember what I'm supposed to be doing?" I whispered to Shayla.

"You're on the boat with Ben." She looked at me. "Are you doing okay?"

I shrugged. "Yeah." I had barely slept the night before and couldn't wait for the shift to be over.

"You ready to go?" Ben asked. "Don't worry, I'll drive the boat."

You'd think after an entire summer I'd have managed to learn to drive the damned boat. Just one more reason why I shouldn't be a full-time ranger.

"You can help the swimmers if they need us."

Even though Nikki had babbled on about how many event participants would be hanging out on the swim beach, the sight of them was overwhelming. In their black wetsuits and swim caps, they almost looked like the group of sea lions I'd seen as a child at Fisherman's Wharf in San Francisco. That paired with the huge sponsor banners and an emcee spinning songs between his random bursts of energy made the whole scene more intense than I had imagined possible.

"Do you think they'll need us?" I asked as we walked down the boat ramp to the dock where our large Boston Whaler ranger boat looked ready to tackle the day.

"Couldn't say. But we can't have anyone drowning today."

We stepped into the boat and fastened our life jackets —the type that inflated once they came into contact with the water.

"I saw your video." Ben turned the key, and the boat roared to life.

I unhooked the ropes securing the boat to the dock, and he pushed the throttle handle forward. "I think everyone saw the video. I'm sorry I made a fool of the rangers."

"Is that what she said to you yesterday?" He shook his head. "At least you tried. Brock stood there terrified after he called you to handle what he should have done himself."

He pulled out into the sectioned-off area where the swimmers would make their way around three massive buoys before returning to the swim beach and running to their bikes in the parking lot.

"Don't worry, kiddo. She'll get over it. Your fifteen minutes of fame will be over once something else becomes more exciting."

I shrugged and pulled my hat down.

The sun was rising over the prairie on the east side of the reservoir when Nikki's voice came over the radio. "Five minutes until the start of the race."

On shore, Nikki stood next to Ursula in the midst of the sea lion people flapping their arms like they were Olympic swimmers ready to earn their gold medals.

"Why don't you pull the dive door so we have easier access to get people out of the water?" Ben said pointing to where a section of the boat's sidewall could be removed.

I unclasped the hinges and pulled it out placing it to the side.

"If someone too large needs assistance, I'll give you

the controls and pull them out. Do you think you'll be able to hold the boat steady if that happens?"

"I think so," I said. Though I hadn't gotten good at maneuvering the boat, I could at least keep it in one place.

The emcee's voice came over the loudspeakers—quieter now that we were on the water—talking about the race and beginning the countdown, "Five, four, three, two, one." The bullhorn blared, echoing through the Marina Cove. Swimmers made a mad dash for the water and entered splashing like hungry sharks were chasing them.

"Keep your eyes peeled for signs of distress." Ben maneuvered the boat to be closer to the swimmers. Lifeguards paddled in kayaks between the swimmers and our boat.

Everyone seemed to be doing okay. Some of the swimmers peeled through the water as if it were as easy as taking a breath while others struggled, splashing with every stroke.

"We have a drowning." Brock's shaky voice came over the radio.

Already? The race had barely begun. The panic in Ben's eyes mirrored my own.

"Where? Where's the drowning?" I called out on the radio frantically searching the water.

"Golden Rock Pond."

"Get off this channel and call the police," Nikki hissed into her mic. I could see the anger on her face all the way from the water.

Ben backed the boat away from the swimmers. "He should have said that in the first place. He knows we have a triathlon going on over here."

"Who is he working with today?"

"Dusty," Ben replied. "Seamus is out here, patrolling the rest of the reservoir while we are stuck on event duty."

"Three bodies in one week." I wiped the sweat from my brow. The sun was up in full force now. "At least I wasn't there for this one."

"Looks like we have our first person in need of help," Ben said and turned the boat in the direction of the start line.

Someone—whether male or female, I couldn't tell due to the swim cap and goggles—flailed only yards from where the race had begun. "That didn't take long," I said.

"Do you think you can help him or her into the boat?"

The person looked to weight at least three hundred pounds. "I'll do my best," I said.

He expertly drove the boat right next to the person so they could hold onto the dive door opening.

"Thank you so much. I don't know what happened," a woman's weak voice said as I grabbed her hands and began to pull. "I trained so hard. But then I thought about the fish and everything below me and the water was so dark. Are you going to pull me in?"

I was trying but making no progress.

"Uh, Ben?"

"Take the controls and try not to let the boat move." He took the woman's hands, and I took the wheel.

I could do this.

He pulled the woman out of the water without so much as a grunt and sat her on the seat before wrapping a blanket around her.

Only about five yards in front of the boat another swimmer called out for help.

"Ben?" I said, but he was busy talking to the woman, making sure she was okay.

I squared my shoulders and pushed the throttle forward turning the wheel like Ben had before. All I had to do was move straight forward.

The boat jolted at the panicking swimmer. Their arms and legs splashed frantically as they tried to get to us.

"Rylie what are you—"

But Ben's warning came too late. The boat came to a grinding stop, and the engine sputtered.

Before I could make a correction, Ben was at the controls trimming up the engine and slamming the boat into reverse. I had driven the boat into the sand.

"Help. Help me," the swimmer yelled.

"Stand up," Ben shouted back. And the swimmer stopped and stood, the water only coming up to their thighs.

Ben revved the engine trying to get the boat out of the sand.

"I'm sorry, Ben. I thought I had it." I looked on shore where Nikki and Ursula watched every move we made. I might as well have unpinned my badge now. Ursula was inevitably going to demand it once I was back on dry land.

"It happens to all of us," Ben reassured me, but his kind words didn't make me feel any better. He didn't know what this meant. I was no longer employed.

He pushed the throttle handle all the way in the back-ward position turning the wheel back and forth—water spluttering from the propeller mere inches below the surface—until finally, we were free.

After pulling four more people into the boat because they were either terrified of the open water or because they were too exhausted to finish, my part of the race—and my stint as a park ranger—was over. It was time to hand over my badge.

The minute I stepped on the dock I was met by a crowd of people, an angry-looking Nikki, and Ursula whose smile was so broad it was almost creepy. She didn't have to look so happy to fire me.

"Rylie, I'm so happy you're here," Ursula roared as she put her arm around my waist and pushed me up the beach towards the plaza area.

Had I lost my hearing? Was she being . . . nice?

"I have some people who want to meet you."

The crowd and Nikki followed behind us as I tried not to trip in the sand.

"Who?" I managed to ask.

"Apparently, you've grown quite a following from that video. Antonio informed me of the visitors flocking to the park—and paying admission—just to get the opportunity to see you," she whispered hurriedly under her breath. "I figure the least you can do after you embarrassed yourself and all of us is bring in additional revenue."

We were on the steps leading up next to the tiki buildings.

"How am I supposed to do that? You're not going to fire me?" I asked.

"Fire you?" She let out a loud laugh as if that were the craziest thing I'd ever say. "Why would I fire you?"

"Um, did you see what I did on the boat?"

"That's neither here nor there. You did no damage."

She couldn't be serious.

As we approached the main office, I saw the cameras and people holding microphones in their hands looking like eagles ready to pounce on an unsuspecting mouse.

Me.

"No. No no no. I can't talk to them." I stopped dead in my tracks. My hair was windblown, and I could feel my face crisping from the sun baking down on me all morning.

"You can and you will if you want to keep your job," she hissed in my ear.

Now she was threatening my job again. This lady needed a serious mental evaluation.

I took a deep breath. One part of me wanted to tell her to shove it, but the other knew I needed this job, at least until I could find another. "Fine." How bad could it be?

"Perfect," she said. "This is Rylie Cooper, or as you all know her, the snake wrangler."

Two women and one man lunged at me with their microphones all spewing questions, their cameramen moving around trying to get the best shot.

"I'm sorry, I didn't get those questions. Could we go one at a time?" I asked.

So we did. I started with one and made my way

through three separate interviews asking the same questions over and over again.

"How did you feel when the snake bit you?"

"Did it hurt?"

"What will you do differently next time?"

Until the very last interview, Ursula stood off to the side but within view nodding in approval at my answers. But when the last news lady asked, "Should visitors be afraid of being attacked by a snake here at Alder Ridge Reservoir," Ursula jumped in and took over.

"Absolutely not. That's why we have rangers like Rylie who are willing to risk their lives for our guests. Currently, Rylie is one of our summer rangers but may soon be full time meaning visitors would be able to see her year round."

I could hear the dollar signs churning in her mind. Did money really change her mind from firing me to hiring me on full time? What would happen when my fifteen minutes had truly expired? Would she just fire me then?

"And cut," the news lady said. "Thank you, Rylie and er—"

"Ursula, Director of Parks and Recreation."

"If you would," Nikki said in a high voice behind me. "Please follow me over to the finish line where we will be handing out awards."

The news people hesitantly followed, and Nikki shot me a glare.

The crowd hadn't followed Nikki and the cameras, but rather looked as if they were waiting for me to hand out more autographs. An idea popped into my mind.

"Did you mean what you said about the full-time position?" I asked loud enough for the people around us to hear. Heads turned from me to her, awaiting her response.

Ursula narrowed her eyes but then smiled. "Of course I meant it. You're one of the best summer rangers we've ever had. As long as the interview process goes well, you'll be able to call yourself a full-time ranger by the end of October."

My heart raced. Another interview with Ursula. Maybe this time she'd ask what I'd do if I woke up as a rattlesnake.

"I should probably get back to the event," Ursula said. "Don't forget to give these nice people your autograph. They've been waiting here all morning."

I took a deep breath and plastered a smile on my face. "Okay, who's first?"

I couldn't help but be excited when Garrett's name popped up on my phone screen Sunday morning to make sure we were still on for the game that afternoon.

I pulled my hair into a ponytail and out the back of my favorite orange Broncos ball cap then put on my Eli Hudson jersey and my favorite pair of light blue jeans. I swiped on far more mascara than necessary for a football game but enough to make my eyes pop from beneath the brim.

"Did you write down all of the details you know about this man so I can find you if you go missing?" My mother asked when I walked up the stairs.

"I sent them to your phone the first time we went on a date."

She pulled out her flip phone and scrolled through the messages. "I must have deleted it." She snapped the phone shut. "Send it again."

"Megan has it. If I go missing, she can send it to you."

"I just hope you don't end up like that girl you found out at the reservoir."

"Mom." I gasped. "I am most certainly not going to end up missing my head. Garrett is a great guy."

"When do I get to meet him?"

"Uh . . . maybe in a few more weeks. We're not that serious yet."

"I still think you should try again with Luke."

"Luke has a girlfriend."

"His mother says they're on the outs."

"You're talking to his mother now?"

"We've reconnected since you and Luke worked on that case together."

"Well, she apparently doesn't know Luke went to the country club to meet Nikki's parents."

"Oh no, we talked about that this morning."

I didn't need to hear this. It was Luke's business, not mine. I was dating Garrett now.

"Do you want to know what she said?"

Yes. "No, it's okay."

"Okay," my mother said in a sure-you-don't voice. "But it sounds like he was absolutely miserable there. Didn't fit in at all."

"I said I didn't want to know." But still, I couldn't help the smile spreading across my face. "I have to go. Love you."

"I love you too. Don't get beheaded."

The light rail was jam-packed with people on their way to the game. It was one of the biggest home games of the season against one of our biggest rivals—the Kansas City Chiefs.

The smell of body odor, beer, and weed permeated the air making me want to cover my nose with my jersey. Thankfully, the weather was perfect for a Broncos win.

When I arrived at the Mile High stop, I moved with the crowd to where I hoped the waterfall and horses were. Excitement palpitated through the air as I passed tailgate parties full of crazy fans. Horsehead hats, full body orange and blue paint, and even a naked man in a barrel with suspenders made up the crowd.

I looked down at my jeans and jersey and contemplated asking for my own face paint to liven up my outfit. Then decided against it for Garrett's sake.

When I finally made it to the horse statues and waterfall, Garrett stood waiting for me with a huge smile on his face. He wore light jeans and a blue jersey, his hair gelled.

"Have you been waiting long?" I asked.

He opened up his arms, and I accepted the invitation for the hug, letting his towering form envelop me for a few seconds. He smelled like bubble gum and Axe body spray.

"Not long at all." He stepped back and handed me my ticket. "You ready?"

It took everything in me not to squeal. A Broncos division game with a hot guy. Yeah, I was ready.

We walked through metal detectors before entering the stadium. Steel and concrete would typically be cold and hard, but as the backdrop of eager fans shuffling to the various concession stands, souvenir shops, and their seats overlooking the field, it was downright cozy.

"Are you hungry? Should we get something to eat before we go to our seats?"

My stomach grumbled on cue. "Sure."

He grabbed my hand and navigated us through the crowd towards a concession vendor.

"I'll take a jumbo dog and some nachos, please," he said then looked down at me for my order.

"You don't have to pay for me." It was only right to offer to pay for myself—I reached into my small cross-body purse for some money, but he had none of it.

"I've got this." His smile could have melted the polar ice caps. "Go ahead."

"I'll take nachos with jalapeños, please."

The man behind the counter busied himself getting our food.

"Do you want a drink too?"

"Maybe just a Coke," I replied.

"Make that two." He handed over money to the cashier. "Let's go find our seats," he said when the food was up.

Our seats were on the fifty-yard line, three rows up from the field.

"Wow, these are great seats," I said.

"The perks of being a nerd, I guess."

The players warmed up on the field, and I could feel my eyes widening. It was surreal being this close to the team I cheered on every week.

"I've arranged for us to meet Eli Hudson after the game."

My head whipped around to meet his gaze, and before I knew it, my lips were on his. After a moment of shock, his lips softened, and his fingers grazed my cheek.

I pulled away. "Sorry, I guess I got excited."

"Don't—you don't have to apologize." His face was bright red. "I'm glad I can make it up to you after my abysmal behavior on our first date."

A piece of hair on his jersey caught my eye. I plucked it off. "I've always heard Huskies shed a lot." I held the hair up for him to see.

"Babbitt is actually an Alaskan Malamute. Easy to mix up. But yes, he sheds a ton."

What was it with me and mixing up animal species?

"It reminds me of my favorite joke." A smile brightened his eyes. "How do you tell an alligator from a crocodile?"

"Do you want the technical answer or—"

"One you'll see later and the other you'll see after a while." His laugh was contagious, and even though the joke was rather dumb, I found myself doubled over in laughter struggling to catch my breath.

The game was amazing. Hudson was on fire throwing touchdown after touchdown.

"You talked about your nieces and nephews at dinner the other night, but you didn't say anything about your siblings. How many do you have?" I asked at halftime.

"Three brothers," he said rubbing his thumb over mine as our fingers intertwined. "They're quite the handful. They're lucky they produce cute kids or I wouldn't have anything to do with them half the time." His hesitant laugh told me he wasn't completely joking.

"Do they get themselves into trouble?" I asked trying not to pry too much but unable to temper my curiosity. I only had one sister who was basically perfect.

"Some. Nothing that gets them arrested or anything but enough to be a frustration."

"Are your parents still together?" I asked before taking a sip of my Coke. Garrett had stuck with soda as well, keeping good on his promise not to get drunk.

"My dad died when we were kids, but Mom's still hanging in there. Her birthday's coming up, and she'll be in town."

"I know, you told me." I chuckled. I had her gift in the back of my car after all.

"Oh, yeah." He rolled his eyes at himself. "But yeah, she's pretty amazing for dealing with four boys all these years. I try to help, but my brothers don't always listen to me. But enough about me, I think you said you had a sister?"

"I do. And she has four boys." I laughed. "She definitely has her hands full, but she takes it all in stride. It's amazing. She's always been the good one. The one who makes my parents proud."

"I'm sure you make them proud too."

I shrugged. "I don't know about proud, but my mom is definitely happy I'm living with them again."

"Oh?" Garrett's voice squeaked. He cleared his throat. "You live with your parents?"

Damn. I hadn't meant to tell him. Not yet anyway. "Uh, yeah. Only for a little while. When I moved down from the mountains after my ex and I broke up, I didn't have enough money to get a place until I found a good job and it looks like I'm going to possibly get the full-time—"

"Whoa." He squeezed my hand. "It's okay. I don't mind that you live with your parents. But it does explain why you didn't want me to pick you up."

I could feel my cheeks warm. "You really don't mind?"

"We all fall on hard times. That's why we have family. No matter what happens, family is supposed to look out for one another."

I sucked in a deep breath trying to calm my racing pulse—thankful he hadn't blown me off. Something about Garrett made me forget about Troy and Antonio and Luke. Well, almost forget Luke.

Garrett spent the rest of the time making me laugh and asking questions about the game. He didn't know much about football, but I didn't mind giving him some insight.

When the last whistle had blown, giving us the win, I found myself sadder about having to move from beneath Garrett's arm than I was about the actual game being over. Cheers surrounded us as Garrett cupped my face in his hands and kissed me.

I wrapped my arms around his neck letting my fingers play in his hair. His tongue darted in and out of my mouth sending sparks down my spine. By the time we pulled ourselves apart, half of the stands had emptied.

"We should probably go down and meet Eli." Garrett

stood and offered a hand to help me up. "Don't want to keep him waiting."

At that point, I would have almost taken another make-out session over meeting the QB. But it was Eli Hudson . . .

We were two of about twenty people led into a back room to meet with Eli. When we stepped in at the end of the line, we were greeted by the devilishly handsome quarterback and four of his bodyguards.

"Thanks for coming." Eli's smile lit up the room. He was even more handsome in person. I squeezed Garrett's hand and looked over at him. His eyes were taking in every part of my face, a smile touching his lips. Eli might have been handsome, but Garrett was more than attractive. He was warm and funny and a damn good kisser.

"Nice jersey," Eli said when we finally made it to the front of the line. I was, of course, wearing his number. "Can I sign it?"

"Yes, please," I managed to say. I'd never been so star struck in my life.

He uncapped his sharpie. "Who can I make it out to?"

"Rylie," I said and then spelled it for him.

He scribbled his message on my back making me shiver.

We posed for a picture, and I congratulated him on his win before the bodyguards ushered Garrett and me out of the room.

"That was so cool. Thank you!" I hugged him.

"You're welcome." He kissed the top of my head. "Did you drive here?"

"No, I took the light rail."

"I can drive you back to your car if you'd like," he said. "Where did you park?"

"Up north. It's pretty far. You really don't have to."

"I want to," he said smiling down at me. He held my hand all the way out of the stadium through the gates and out to the parking lot where a brand new dark green Toyota Corolla sat all alone. He opened my door for me and then went around to get in on his side.

The car was immaculate just like his house, minus a few dog hairs here and there from his *Alaskan Malamute*. "Do you take Babbitt with you a lot?"

"Yeah, he goes with me practically everywhere. He's my bud. Sorry about the hair."

"No problem, Fizzy sheds too."

"When do I get to meet this Fizzy?" he asked turning in his seat to face me.

"Introducing our kids so soon?" I gave a joking grin. "We could take them to the dog park sometime. Fizzy would love that."

"It's a date." He chuckled and slid his hand onto my knee rubbing it with his thumb.

Before we could say anything else, we were kissing again. I don't know who made the move, but the kissing turned into a full-blown make-out session within seconds.

His hands ran up under my jersey, caressing my back and pulling me closer to him over the center console. He showered my neck in increasingly eager kisses as I maneuvered my hips closer to him. I pulled his shirt from the waistband of his pants and ran my fingers over his slightly-squishy stomach when it sounded like the glass on the driver's side window exploded.

We separated like two kids caught making out at lover's point.

"What was that?" I asked smoothing my hair.

Garrett didn't answer but instead rolled down his window. "Can I help you?"

"Garrett Henry?" An angry voice came from outside.

"Yes, that's me," Garrett replied.

"I need you to step out of the car. Now." It wasn't a request.

Garrett opened his door and got out. Before he could close the door, I heard the loud thump of Garrett's body hitting the side of the car.

I threw my door open and jumped out ready to fight someone when I made eye contact with none other than Luke.

My mind was fuzzy as Luke said to Garrett, "You're under arrest for the murder of Alex Johnson."

"Murder?" Garrett's face went ashy. "No way. I don't even know an Alex Johnson."

"His friends call him Boy Boy," Luke barked.

Garrett looked at me pleading. "I'm so sorry. There must be a mistake."

"It's okay. I'm sure they've got the wrong person." I glared at Luke.

Luke ignored me and began reading Garrett his Miranda rights.

"Oh come on, there's no way he killed anyone." My voice pleading now.

Garrett looked like a scared puppy left in a cardboard box on the side of the road in the pouring rain.

"Do you understand these rights as I've explained them to you?" Luke finished.

Garret nodded.

"I need a verbal yes or no," Luke said through gritted teeth still holding Garrett against the Corolla.

"Yes, I understand." Garrett's voice was quiet.

Luke pulled him from the side of the Corolla and ushered him to the police car where Jerry stood holding the door open.

My mind reeled. How could they think Garrett killed Boy Boy? And Boy Boy was dead?

"Wait. Rylie." Garrett turned to me. "I'm sorry. I don't know what's happening. I didn't kill anyone."

"I know," I replied. "It's all a misunderstanding."

"Can you take care of Babbitt?" Garrett asked as he was lowered into the cruiser.

"Yes, of course," I said.

"Take my keys. You can take the car to your car and then leave it at the lot. I'll take care of it when I get this all figured out. Just take care of Babbitt."

"I will. It'll all be—" but before I could finish the sentence, Luke slammed the door in Garrett's face.

He turned to me with a look of disgust. "You have a hickey on your neck."

My hand shot up to where Garrett's lips had been moments before.

"I don't know how you've conjured up Garrett as a suspect."

"He has you to thank for that."

"Me? How—"

But Luke wasn't listening anymore. He got into the

driver's seat of the patrol car, put the car in drive, and tore out of the parking lot.

I fought the urge to stick my tongue out at him as they drove away. I had to figure out what Luke was talking about. How could I have been the one to make Garrett a suspect?

15

The clock on Garrett's dash read 7:20 when I finally pulled out of the parking lot. It had taken a minute for me to get my wits about me. I yanked my cell phone from my purse and called Shayla.

"Hello?"

"Shay? It's Rylie." I pulled onto the Interstate and wove my way over to the fast lane. The Corolla was no Cherry Anne, but it had spunk.

"Hey, Ry, what's up? How'd your date go?"

"It was fine until Luke arrested Garrett." My voice sounded angrier than I intended.

"What?" I could hear her readjust the phone. "Why would Luke arrest Garrett?"

"For murder. Luke thinks Garrett killed Boy Boy." I took a breath. "I didn't even know Boy Boy was dead."

"Didn't you watch the news this morning?" Shayla said. "That's the body Brock and Dusty found over at Golden Rock Pond."

"But—"

"And remember you saw two people in Garrett's boat that day?"

Dammit. I hit the steering wheel with my palm. "Did Seamus tell the police?"

"He didn't have to." Her voice turned angry. "*You* told Luke yourself."

I racked my brain. Had I told Luke? No. Why would I have?

"Sorry, I didn't mean to insult your *boyfriend*," I hissed.

"He's not—why would you—" Shayla sounded like she might cry. "How did you know?"

"I could tell the other day," I said in a softened tone. "It's okay, I won't say anything."

"Was it really that obvious?"

"Maybe not to everyone, but I'm your best friend. And speaking of, why didn't you tell me?"

"We didn't want to get in trouble for fraternizing and since the season's almost over and I'll hopefully be going off to police academy, we decided to wait to go public."

"Makes sense."

"But enough about me. What about Garrett? Do you think he did it?"

When I'd met him on the boat ramp, I would have said it was possible, but after the day we had there was no way. "No. He couldn't have. He's probably one of the nicest people I've ever met. He even set up a meeting with Eli Hudson—er—the quarterback."

"Wow. He must have really liked you."

"Don't talk like he's dead. He does really like me, and I really like him too." I turned off the Interstate onto the exit to Garrett's house. "Luke caught us totally making out."

"No." Shayla gasped.

"Yep. In the car. Like freakin' teenagers."

She giggled. "I bet Luke was pissed."

"Oh, he was," I said. "Are you busy right now?"

"Not really . . ."

"Is Seamus with you?"

She hesitated before answering. "Yes."

"Can you leave him for a bit and come pick me up from Garrett's house and take me to my car?"

"Wait, you're at Garrett's house?"

I could hear Seamus in the background say, "Tell her that's not a good idea."

"Yes, I'm here to take care of his dog. I figured I'd drop his car off too."

"Where does he live?"

I gave her the address, and she said she'd be over in about an hour. Just enough time for me to take care of Babbitt and do a little snooping around.

———

I pulled the car into the garage to the right of the truck and the boat. It wasn't like most people's garages—untidy with stuff everywhere. It was almost as clean as his house. I could hear Babbitt crying from inside, so I decided to let him out before I snooped.

The stairs leading up to the house from the garage were only wide enough to hold one person, and when I opened the door, Babbitt nearly toppled me backward down them.

"Whoa, buddy. Chill out." I patted the top of his head. "You're okay."

Poor guy needed to pee so badly, he almost did it on the floor right then and there. Thankfully, I got him out into the fenced backyard in time. A fancy ceramic container that matched the kitchen décor held gourmet dog food.

At the sound of food hitting his bowl, Babbitt raced back to the house and shoved his head into the bowl, furiously attacking the bits of dog food gold.

While Babbitt ate, I decided to take a look around. I was careful not to touch anything as I made my way up the stairs and into what looked to be a guest bedroom. The smell of lavender and vanilla pricked at my senses. A delicate white bedspread with tiny purple flowers covered the queen-sized bed. Two white nightstands sat on either side framing the white Victorian style headboard. Other than an alarm clock, the stands were completely void of items.

The room had a walk-in closet and a private bathroom. The medicine cabinet was as bare as the one downstairs.

I moved on.

My heart raced when I stood in front of what I assumed to be Garrett's bedroom door. The pitter-patter of dog paws up the hardwood stairs alerted me to Babbitt's presence. His eyes were accusatory as he sat next to me.

"I know, I shouldn't be doing this. But I'm trying to help," I said as much to convince him as myself. "Don't you want your daddy back?" What could I possibly find to clear his name? There was only one way to find out.

"Here goes nothing," I said.

Babbitt let out a low howl.

I turned the doorknob, and the heavy door swung open without a sound. The smell of Garrett's cologne wafted over me sending chills up my neck where his kisses had been only hours before.

The room was enormous, almost as big as the apartment I'd shared with my ex. The king-sized bed sat pushed up against a wall with a picture window to one side framing what I guessed would be a great view of the mountains past the city skyline that looked like Christmas lights against the dark sky.

He had to have paid a fortune for this house.

I inched my way into the room, my Adidas leaving footprints in the freshly vacuumed white carpet. Two doors stood regally on the opposite wall leading to what I assumed to be a bathroom and closet.

Starting with the bathroom, I pulled my shirtsleeve over my hand and turned the doorknob. The main focal point of the meticulously clean granite and white room was a circular jet tub, but even the toilet was spotless.

Was this man inhuman? Did he not pee? I'd never seen a cleaner bathroom.

The lighted mirrors atop the granite countertop with a turquoise glass bowl sink didn't have cabinets behind them. I opened a drawer to find hand towels rolled neatly next to a soap dish and an unwrapped but unused bar of soap.

Moving on to each drawer, I became more and more

frustrated. Everything looked untouched. The toothbrush was in perfect condition, the toothpaste still plump, and there were absolutely zero pill bottles matching the ones I'd seen before.

Not only did something seem off, but I was starting to doubt the possibility of having a relationship with this man. There was no way Garrett would want to live with me if things got more serious. I wasn't messy per se, but I definitely wouldn't be able to keep up with this level of cleanliness.

Babbitt stood at the edge of the doorway, not stepping a paw into the room when I emerged from the bathroom.

"What's going on here?" I asked him.

He tilted his head to the side and let out a low growl.

"I know, you don't want me in here but—"

Woof!

His bark made me jump.

"Okay, okay. I'm done." Inside at least. There was a still a boat and truck I needed to check out.

16

W hen I opened the door of the truck, a wafting of stale power bait and a faint hint of a woman's perfume hit me in the face. I searched through the thoroughly dirty vehicle only to find a pair of broken sunglasses, several empty beer cans, and a lacy black bra that would come closer to fitting Carmen's Dolly-sized boobs than my own almost-B cup.

Was Garrett seeing someone else? And why in the world would any girl take off their bra in such a disgusting vehicle? There were trash wrappers on the floor, a layer of dust on the dash thicker than Nikki's fake acrylic nails, and honestly, it smelled like something—or someone— had died in there. The thought of Garrett stepping foot in this trash heap didn't fit. I had to be missing something.

I snapped pictures with my phone and moved onto the boat. I pushed myself up on the wheel well of the boat trailer and swung one leg after the other over the side. Careful not to disturb too much, I picked through the various items of clothing thrown about. The black duffel bag was missing, but the tackle box was still half-open with the prescription bottles lying inside.

He hadn't even taken them in with him? He had to have another stash unless he didn't actually take them regularly.

I took a step up onto the bench seat to get a closer look at the prescriptions bottles, but as I pushed off, my foot slipped out from under me, and I landed hard on the metal hull. The seat I had been standing on had been dislodged, disclosing a hidden storage box.

I rolled over onto my knees and rubbed my butt—convinced I'd broken my tailbone—before peering into the open storage container. Bundle upon bundle of hundred dollar bills were lined up neatly in rows, completely encased in plastic.

What the hell? Was he involved with Boy Boy after all? My heart raced at the thought.

But I knew Garrett. He was a good guy. A sweet guy. There's no way he'd kill someone. Was there?

I shook my head. No. There was an explanation. There had to be an explanation. Maybe he kept his money in his boat instead of in the bank. I knew lots of people who didn't trust the bank. Maybe he was one of them.

When I replaced the seat to cover the money, I heard a car pull into the driveway. My heart raced. Had Luke already gotten a warrant?

My eyes darted to the pill bottles. I didn't have time to take photos. Instead, I shoved them into my pocket, jumped out of the boat, and ran up the stairs only to find I'd somehow managed to lock myself out of the house.

Shit.

The only exit other than the door to the driveway was a small window leading to the backyard, but it was above a workbench covered in tools and various car parts and—even if I could reach it—I'd likely get stuck trying to get through.

Plan B, I needed a place to hide. If Luke found me in the garage, he'd know I had been snooping around. I didn't need to be hauled into jail for tampering with a crime scene.

Finally, I saw a large cabinet in a corner next to the boat. I silently willed it to be empty as I tiptoed over.

"This is the police, we have a warrant to search this property," Luke said on the other side of the garage door.

Besides a pair of greasy overalls and an old pair of boots, the closet had just enough space for me to squeeze in. I had barely pulled the door closed when two sets of footsteps walked in.

"That looks like the boat and truck Seamus described," Luke's voice made the blood in my face boil. "And somehow he got his car back here already." Luke paused as if contemplating the thought.

"Maybe your girlfriend brought it back for him."

Boots up the stairs to the house door sounded and then several knocks. "Rylie?" Luke's voice was loud and demanding. "Are you here?"

I expected Babbitt to bark, but no sound came from the other side of the door.

More knocking. "Rylie, if you're here, you need to come out."

Yeah no. I didn't *need* to do anything.

He paused a few seconds.

"Let's get on with it," Jerry croaked.

"I'll take the boat," Luke said. "You take the truck."

"Deal."

It seemed like they searched forever. After a while, I worried I'd topple out of the cupboard from lost feeling in my legs. I expected Luke to yell to Jerry that he'd found a whole crap-ton of money but nothing came.

"Find anything good?" Jerry finally asked, startling me so much I wondered if I'd started to doze off.

"Not really," Luke replied. "Too bad too. I wanted to throw away the key on this guy."

I wanted to burst from the cabinet and throw something at him.

"Yeah. He's not talking, and his attorney's that one who gets all the bad guys off. How'd your girlfriend find this guy?"

"You know I'm dating Nikki."

"Like that's gonna last. You and I both know why you're dating her."

Please don't say it. I didn't know if I could handle hearing how he was just in it for her gorgeous body.

"Nikki's a nice girl when you get to know her," Luke replied with less confidence. "And I think Rylie met him on Tinder or something."

"That makes sense. Look what I found in his truck."

Luke let out a low whistle. The bra.

"Maybe you should warn her about guys on that site."

"You don't know Rylie. She doesn't listen to anyone but herself. The more I tell her not to date him, the more she'll want to."

He was probably right about that.

"Plus, they seem pretty serious already. He gave her the keys to his house and asked her to take care of his dog," Luke said.

"Maybe he doesn't have anyone else to take care of it."

Luke let out a non-commitmental grunt. "What do I care anyway? We've gone our own ways."

My heart constricted. Had we? He said it with such finality. I swallowed down the tightness and took a deep breath.

"I just hope she's not dating a murderer."

"You don't?" Jerry asked. "A second ago you said you'd like this guy to go away for a long time."

"Just because we're not together doesn't mean I want her in danger."

"The only way to keep her from dating other guys is to date her yourself. Annoying as she is, she's still hot."

I didn't know whether to be offended or flattered.

"I'm done talking about it." Luke sounded frustrated. "Let's finish this up so we can search the house."

"I think I'm done here," Jerry said.

Their footsteps landed heavy on the locked door to the house.

Someone jiggled the knob before I heard a boot slam into the door and splintering of the wooden doorframe.

I hoped Babbitt wasn't directly behind it.

"That's one way to get in," Jerry said.

Luke was silent.

I waited for them to make their way into the house before I managed to extricate myself from the closet doing a few high kicks to shake the tingles from my legs. The pill bottles rattling around in my pockets made my conscience squirm.

The door to the house was wide open, and there was no sound of a dog inside. Where had Babbitt gone?

I let myself out of the garage and figured I'd be safe getting in through the back door. Hopefully, Luke would think I had been outside taking Babbitt for a walk or something.

The houses were so close together it was almost impossible to walk between them without looking into the neighbor's window.

Thankfully, Garrett's neighbors kept their curtains drawn.

When I got around to the backyard, the back door was wide open.

"Babbitt?" I called out. Maybe he was still in the house?

I walked up to the back door and into the house. "Babbitt?" I called again not caring if Luke heard me this time. Babbitt still didn't come to me.

"Excuse me, miss," Jerry said, his eyes widening at the sight of me. "What are you doing here?"

"Taking care of Garrett's dog like he asked me to." I put my hands on my hips. "What are you doing here?"

"We got a search warrant and I ain't seen no dog. But you can't be here."

No dog? Where had Babbitt gone? It was dark outside. How was I going to find him? Garrett would never forgive me for losing his dog.

"Are you sure you haven't seen a dog?"

"Nope. Hey Luke, you seen a dog anywhere?" Jerry called up the stairs.

"No dog. No evidence. Nothing," Luke said walking back down the stairs, his gaze focusing on me and then narrowing. "What are you doing here?"

"Taking care of Garrett's dog like I promised," I said returning his stare.

"Not doing a very good job if you don't even know where the dog is," Jerry said. And we both shot him looks of disgust. "Whoa sorry." He held his hands up in surrender. "I'll get the tow trucks on the phone to take the boat and the truck into impound."

Luke nodded.

"Wait, impound? Why can't you search them here?"

"We did," Luke said. "But it's protocol. The lab will need to go over them with a fine tooth comb since we think they're the location of at least one murder."

They'd find the money, but there wasn't anything I could do to stop it without setting off Luke's internal lie detector.

"You didn't touch anything before we got here, did you?"

Only everything. "Uh, yeah. I touched the dog food and the doors, oh and I've been here before so I'm sure my fingerprints are all over the place."

The hurt in his eyes made my stomach sour, but how else would I explain the possibility of my fingerprints being in Garrett's bedroom? I'd been careful, but I still could have touched something. Plus hadn't he told Jerry we were over minutes before?

"Fine, but you need to stay out while we search. And

speaking of search, maybe you should look for the dog. Your boyfriend"—he practically choked on the word —"won't be happy if you lost his best friend."

I thought of how I'd feel if someone lost Fizzy and tears sprung to my eyes. I had to find Babbitt. "Are you sure he's not upstairs somewhere?"

"Not that I saw." Luke shrugged.

I turned and marched back out into the backyard. "Babbitt?" I cried out, my voice giving away the panic flowing through my veins. If only it weren't dark, then I could see. I decided to search the perimeter of the fence for places he might have been able to escape. "Babbitt?"

"Rylie?" Shayla's voice came from behind me making me jump a foot off the ground.

"Shayla, you scared the shit out of me." I took a breath trying to steady my nerves.

"I'm sorry. I didn't mean to. What are you doing?"

"I think I lost Garrett's dog."

"It's okay. We'll find him." She started calling. "Did you talk to Luke?"

"Yeah, he's still inside."

She nodded. "Jerry was directing the tow trucks to take the boat and the truck from the garage."

"They're impounding them because they think they might be the crime scene."

"Maybe we should start searching the neighborhood," Shayla said.

Panic was turning into dread. How would we ever find an Alaskan Malamute on the run? He was probably halfway to—well—Alaska by now.

"Hey, Rylie?" Luke's voice came from the doorway.

139

"Yeah?" I turned around.

"I think I found the dog." He motioned for me to follow him and said a quick hello to Shayla as we walked back into the house.

The way he'd said it made me think Babbitt had been run over by a car or something. But when we got inside, he was curled up in a tight ball on the couch.

"I thought he was a pillow until I took a closer look," Luke said.

I dropped to my knees and threw my arms around Babbitt's neck as he kissed my face. "I'm so glad we found you. I'm not letting you out of my sight again."

Luke turned and walked away.

Shayla laughed. "How about I take you to your car now?"

"Babbitt is coming with, is that okay?" I hurriedly added, "If not, I can come back and pick him up after I get my car."

"Of course it's okay," Shayla said.

Shayla said goodbye to Luke, and I threw up a wave before we went on our way.

After Shayla dropped Babbitt and me off at Cherry Anne, I pulled out the two orange bottles from my pocket that read G. Henry and with an expiration date a month out.

Babbitt nudged my hand with his nose and let out a low growl.

"I know, I shouldn't have these, but I'm trying to help. I promise."

Babbitt turned and began to investigate the back seat with his nose scratching at the leather now and then while

I Googled the names on the bottles—Zineclara and Oretaline. I'd never heard of either medication. All of the fancy medical terminology on my screen made my head spin. I clicked off my phone. I'd have to do some more digging to figure out what they were for, but at the moment I just wanted to get home and curl up in bed.

17

The news of Boy Boy's murder was all over my parents' television screen when I woke up the next morning. Babbitt and Fizzy had become fast friends and didn't move at all when I got out of bed to go upstairs.

My father sat in his leather recliner reading his morning paper and drinking his black coffee while my mother got ready to go to work.

"And this man," a photo flashed on the screen next to the news anchor, "Garrett Henry, has been taken into custody as a suspect."

My eyes felt like they might pop out of my head. Garrett's mugshot was terrible. His eyes looked like he'd been crying and his hair was all messed up—whether from our makeout sesh or from Luke's rough handling, I couldn't tell.

"Wait, what did the TV say?" My mother emerged

from the hall bathroom where she had been applying her makeup.

"Nothing. It said nothing." She knew Garrett's name. If she found out I was dating a suspected murderer, she'd lose her mind.

"I'll back it up for you." My father held up the remote and hit the rewind button. Why did TV have to be so sophisticated?

The news reporter repeated her story about Boy Boy and Garrett, my mother's eyes growing until they became as large as dinner plates.

"That-that's—" She turned her attention to me, one finger pointed at the TV screen. "That's the man you went out with yesterday."

"No, it's just—"

"Don't you lie to me, young lady." Her voice was the same pitch it had been when I'd come home at four in the morning on my eighteenth birthday declaring I was no longer bound by her rules. "I know *exactly* who that is. I stalked him on the Facebook."

I stopped myself from pointing out it was called Facebook, not *the* Facebook. "It's a big misunderstanding."

"So you *are* dating that man?" my father asked, his voice thick with concern.

"Yes. But he's not a killer." I added quickly. "He's a really nice guy who Luke decided to arrest."

"Luke arrested him?" Mom yelled. "If Luke thinks he's bad, Rylie, then he most certainly is."

The pitter-patter of two dogs running up the stairs mixed with my mother's hysterics.

"Luke also thought Dave killed Ronnie and he was wrong," I reminded her.

"I don't want you seeing him," my mother managed to say.

"Well, it's kinda hard to date a guy in jail," I joked, trying to lighten the mood.

"Don't sass your mother," Dad said. "She's only looking out for what's best for you."

"Wait where did that dog come from?" Mom's finger pointed directly at a happy-faced Babbitt.

"That's Garrett's dog. I'm taking care of him while Garrett's . . ."

"In prison," Mom said.

"In jail," I corrected. "It was late when I got in last night. I didn't think you'd mind."

"Of course I don't mind." She patted Babbitt on the head. "But I want you to stay completely out of this investigation. The last time you worked a murder, you almost died." She choked on the last word. "I will never get over the phone call telling me my daughter is in the hospital after an attempted murder."

My heart dropped at the tears in her eyes. "Don't worry, Mom. Garrett is innocent. I'll try to stay out of it, but shouldn't I at least help the police with what I know?"

"Luke can handle the investigation, sweetie," Dad said.

I couldn't argue with my dad like I could with my mom. I nodded. I'd be careful. They'd never have to know I helped clear Garrett's name. And once his name was cleared, I'd invite him over to meet them.

"I'd like to visit an inmate," I said to the woman behind the bulletproof glass at the local jail.

"Visiting hours are almost over, maybe you should come back tomorrow." Her eyes were bored as if she had no interest in her job whatsoever.

"I only need five minutes, I promise."

"Fine. Whatever. Which inmate?"

"Garrett Henry."

A smile breached her face. "You Rylie?"

"Uh, yeah." How did she know?

"Luke told me you might show up. Sit down over there, I'll come getcha when Garrett's ready."

I sat in one of the hard plastic chairs lining a brick wall. The air was stale and cool and smelled like cleaning solution. Everything around me was hard—from the concrete floor to the steel doors.

A loud buzzing sound came from a door leading to what I assumed to be the cells. With a click, the door swung open, and the receptionist motioned for me to follow her.

I stood and walked down a long brick hallway back to a small closet-type room with a chair, a pane of glass, and an old-fashioned telephone with the heavy metal-wrapped cord. Garrett sat behind the glass holding his phone up to his ear. A smile breached his lips but didn't reach his eyes.

"Five minutes," she said and slammed the door closed.

I picked up the receiver. "Garrett? Can you hear me?"

He nodded. "Loud and clear."

Seeing him in an orange jumpsuit with a guard hovering behind him made my stomach turn. "How are you?"

"Hanging in there," he said. "How's Babbitt?"

"He's great. I thought I lost him yesterday, but he was on the couch."

"He's pretty lazy," Garrett said.

"I hope you don't mind, but I took him home with me. I couldn't stand the thought of him being there all by himself."

Garrett smiled. "Of course I don't mind. Are he and Fizzy getting along well?"

"Like they've been BFF's for their entire lives."

"Good." Garrett looked as relieved as he could while being incarcerated.

"So you know when we first met?" I asked, not wanting to spoil the mood but needing to ask him my question.

"Rylie," Garrett said shaking his head. "Just so you know they record every conversation I have in here other than with my attorney, so anything we talk about could be held against me."

Damn. So I couldn't ask him about the boat and the pills and the money. Not outright anyway.

"Okay."

"But yes, I remember when we first met. When I was fishing on the boat, right?"

"Yeah."

"And you thought I was up to something?"

I didn't want to say anything more than what Luke already knew. "I did."

"You thought there was another person in my boat from what I can tell after being questioned all night."

"I did. And I'm sorry. I know now it was probably a trick of the light or—"

"Don't apologize for doing your job." Even behind bars, he was full of kindness. "I can tell you there are more factors to this than I can explain, but my attorney knows what's going on and he's working on getting me out of here."

"But I can help. I want to help. I know about the boat," I blurted out. "They impounded it. All of it."

Garrett's brows knitted together in the middle of his forehead. "You don't need to help, Rylie. I don't want to put you in danger. I didn't kill Boy Boy, but someone did, and that person is still out there. If you're sticking your nose into this, he or she might come after you."

"But I—"

"No. Please. Just take care of Babbitt for me. That's all the help I need. I have a fantastic attorney and a clear conscience. Everything is going to be fine, Rylie. Trust me."

"Have they set your bail?"

"Not yet. I have my hearing this afternoon, but as soon as the judge determines the amount, I'll post bail and be back on the outside."

The receptionist had returned and impatiently tapped her toe behind me. "I think my time is up."

"I'll see you this evening," Garrett smiled. "Maybe we can order in?"

I nodded and tried to return his smile. "Sounds perfect."

"You know, he's pretty cute for a murderer," the receptionist said as she led me back to the front of the building.

"Not only is he good looking, but he's also a great guy. And he's not a murderer."

"Not as great as Luke, though. That man, mmmm." She was practically salivating. "I'm surprised you let him get away. If I had a chance with him, I'd—"

"Luke's dating someone."

"Nikki," she rolled her eyes, "I know. She's a peach."

"I work with her."

"I hear they're only dating because—"

"Because why?" Luke asked as we nearly ran headlong into him when we rounded a corner.

Her face turned an almost purple shade of red. "No-no reason. Because you like each other, of course." She tried to regain her composure.

"Of course." Luke let out a laugh. "Thanks for taking Rylie back, I'll escort her to her car."

The receptionist looked as if she might pass out from Luke's smile.

"I can walk to my car alone, thanks," I said.

"I need to talk to you."

"I think we've done enough talking the last few days." I pushed open the heavy glass doors leading to the parking lot, not bothering to hold them open for Luke.

"Garrett isn't who you think he is."

I turned on a dime coming nose to nose with the man I'd kissed only months before. The man I'd wanted a relationship with but who turned me down because he didn't want to be my rebound. Now I wanted to punch him in the mouth more than kiss him on it.

"How do you know who Garrett is?"

"Because I interrogated him last night." The bags under his gorgeous brown eyes verified his story.

"And what did you find out?"

Luke looked down at the ground. "I can't tell you that."

I let out a grunt of anger and frustration. "Then why are you even talking to me?"

I turned towards Cherry Anne, but Luke grabbed my arm and spun me back around to face him. "Because I care about you, Rylie. I don't want you to get hurt."

I cursed the butterflies that always danced in my stomach when I was in such close proximity to Luke. "Do you really think Garrett is going to hurt me?"

Luke started to talk but then stopped himself. "I don't know." He admitted. He loosened his grip on my arm, but his fingers still rested on my skin.

"So then why—"

"There are things you don't know." He dropped his hand to his side. "This case is a mess. It's dangerous. And your boyfriend isn't making it any easier. What we do know is Boy Boy was head of a gang—a horrible gang. A gang that will stop at nothing to keep their secrets."

"I don't know their secrets. I'm in no danger." I crossed my fingers behind my back. The money alone was a big enough secret to kill over. If it was gang money which it probably wasn't.

"But if you keep poking your nose in places it doesn't belong, you might come across something you don't even know is a secret. Please stop."

"How did Boy Boy die?" I blurted out.

"Boy Boy had toxic levels of prescription medication in his bloodstream which could have impaired his ability to swim causing him to drown."

My mind rushed to the nearly empty pill bottles in my glove compartment. "So he wasn't dead when he went in the water?" My insides clenched. I could have saved him.

Luke shook his head. "Nope. Not that I should be telling you this. God, why do I tell you these things?" He turned and stormed back towards the station. "Just stay out of trouble." He yelled not looking back at me.

Yeah, not likely.

I had a couple of hours to spare before I had to be in for my shift, so I decided to take Fizzy and Babbitt to the dog park to get rid of some of their energy.

The dog park consisted of what I assume was at one time a patch of grass but was now dirt surrounded by a wire and log fence with various play features within. I had taken Fizzy here a handful of times, but every time he nearly pulled me over to get inside. Babbitt, on the other hand, stayed close by my side, not wanting to join the group.

Dogs of all shapes and sizes ran around playing and jumping and rolling in only God knows what. Bose headphone guy with the mastiff was busy with his phone, bobbing his head slightly to a beat only he could hear. The bronze goddess, who looked like she spent several hours a day in the tanning booth, held her fluffy white poodle in her lap as they watched the dogs play around them. And the white-haired, hunched old woman who would yell for her Mitzy so loudly the entire park could hear waved at me.

Though we were all there for the same reason, we never seemed to talk. We just let our doggies play while we sipped our lattes and enjoyed the sunshine.

"Why don't you go play, Babbitt?" I asked. I only knew the two commands Garrett had done the night I'd been at his house—stay and sick—and neither of them fit quite right with this situation.

"Run," I said.

Babbitt just stared up at me with his sky blue eyes.

"Go?" I asked.

Nothing.

I looked out finding Fizzy smelling the butt of an old Boston terrier. "Oh Fizzy," I said under my breath.

"Do you want to play fetch?" I pulled a ball from my pocket.

Babbitt let out a low growl, his ears perking up but his eyes weren't focused on me, they were pointed at the gate where we'd come in.

About six people stood where he was looking. Some were coming, and some were going. All seemed to have dogs, except one.

A person with a baggie zip-up sweatshirt walked outside of the fence perimeter, the hood pulled tightly against their face with their head pointed at the ground. It was this person Babbitt was watching and growling at.

"What's wrong? You don't like people in hoodies?" I asked. The person did look pretty shady.

Babbitt continued to growl.

The person looked up from the ground to reveal a pale

face almost entirely hidden by huge dark sunglasses. They were too far away at this point for me to determine if it was a man or a woman.

"Should we go check it out?" I asked.

Apparently, that was Babbitt's cue to take off. He ran like he was in the race of his life towards the fence.

"No. No Babbitt," I yelled sprinting after him not sure what he would do when he got to the person.

I could feel eyes around me watching. Other dogs chased after Babbitt like it was one big game. Even Fizzy joined in the fun.

But Babbitt was on a mission.

When the person realized the dog was heading right for them, they darted away from the fence and disappeared into the parking lot.

Babbitt was still barking and growling when I reached the fence. A silver car tore out of the parking lot, probably with the person who Babbitt had tried to attack.

"Babbit stop," I yelled. "Sit."

Babbitt instantly stopped barking and sat, his eyes shifting between the fence and me.

The other dogs looked confused before their owners caught up with us. I snapped a leash to Babbitt's collar and then another to Fizzy's.

"I'm sorry. We're leaving," I said to the group of people standing with their arms crossed over their chests throwing judgmental looks my way. The number one rule of the dog park was to never bring a vicious or aggressive dog.

But how was I to know Babbitt would react so strongly to someone in a hoodie?

I made a mental note to talk to Garrett about it when I saw him that night.

"Let's go guys," I said, and Babbitt and Fizzy both trotted next to me as I stormed back to the car, more embarrassed than I'd been since I'd sat in that little girl's sand castle.

The sun was high, but the air was cooler than usual when I arrived at the reservoir. Fall was finally approaching.

"How are you?" Shayla asked when I met her in the plaza area.

"I'm okay. I visited Garrett this morning. He seems to be holding up. Then I took Babbitt and Fizzy to the dog park which ended in disaster."

"Oh no. Doggie drama?"

"Kinda. Babbitt went nuts when he saw someone in a hoodie. We basically got kicked out."

"Kicked out of a dog park. That's gotta be a first." She patted me on the shoulder. "Have you heard from Luke?"

I glanced out at the small crowd of teenagers who were likely on their lunch breaks from the school just outside the walk-in gates. "I saw him this morning after I talked to Garrett. He told me to stay out of the investigation."

Shayla put her hands on her hips. "Haven't I told you that a hundred times already?"

I ignored her comment. "Do you know anything about Zineclara and Oretaline?"

Shayla looked at me with a skeptical glare but before she could answer a voice came from behind us.

"Did I hear someone say Zineclara and Oretaline?" Carmen came bobbing up behind us, from the deck area around the main office.

"Yeah, do you know anything about them?" I asked.

"Sure do. I used to work at a pharmacy. They're anti-anxiety drugs."

Anti-anxiety? Garrett seemed like the least anxious person I knew. Probably because of the medications.

"You don't look happy with that answer," Carmen said her gum smacking between her teeth.

"It wasn't what I was expecting." If I'd dug deeper on Google, I probably could have figured that out myself.

"Why are you asking about prescription medication?" Shayla asked.

"No reason. I was just curious."

"You know, now that I think about it, those two drugs when taken together are sometimes used for multiple personalities."

My ears felt like they perked up. "Multiple personalities?"

"Yep." She nodded vigorously. "I knew this guy once, came into the pharmacy all the time to get them, but sometimes he was Tom and others he was Damon. If he came in as Damon, we'd have to ask to speak to Tom to fill his prescription. He'd snap right over to Tom. It was the strangest thing."

My head spun. Did Garrett have another personality? Could his other personality have killed Boy Boy?

"You don't think Garrett—" Shayla started, but I cut her off with a look.

"No. This has nothing to do with the investigation that

I'm not sticking my nose into." I shifted from one foot to another.

Carmen shrugged. "Too bad that guy you were dating was a killer. From his pictures on TV, he looked pretty hot."

Carmen was the last person I'd let judge the hotness of a guy. She dated nasty creepy Dave.

"I don't think he killed anyone. He was so nice on our date."

"Maybe he didn't kill Boy Boy." Carmen shrugged. "But I'm not sad Boy Boy's dead."

I wish I could say the same. Not that I wanted a big gang member running around killing people, but I couldn't shake the feeling that I should have done more to save him. A life was a life after all.

"Did you hear they finally posted Kyle's position?" Carmen asked.

My mind flipped from Boy Boy to my future. "No. I didn't know."

"It's on the city website. Come see." Carmen led Shayla and me into the park office. She pulled up a tab on her computer and there it was the full-time position listing. I scanned eagerly down the page looking at all the qualifications needed checking them off in my head as I went.

"Is this open to the public or just internally?"

"Looks like its open to the public. But didn't Ursula practically say you had the job on television?"

I didn't trust Ursula to stick with any promises she made whether on TV or not. My fifteen minutes of fame was quickly coming to an end meaning my profitability was too. If I didn't act quickly, I might not have a chance after all.

"Do you mind if I work on my application a little bit this afternoon?" I asked Shayla.

"Nah, it's a slow day. I'll call you if I need you." She turned to walk out of the office then turned back. "And Rylie?"

"Yeah?" I asked.

"Please stay away from the murder investigation."

"I will," I lied.

Shayla frowned as if she didn't believe me, but with Carmen standing right there, she probably didn't want to get into it too much.

"I'll be in the back office," I said to Carmen. "Thanks for giving me a heads up on the position."

"Sure thing." She gave me a toothy grin. "And don't worry, if your guy does have multiple personalities it'll almost be like dating multiple guys. Could be an adventure." She winked.

I laughed nervously. I had no interest in dating someone with a personality that could kill someone.

I hit the submit key from my laptop at home that evening saying a quick prayer that my application would be looked upon favorably and then pulled out my cell phone. Tinder had paired me with a bunch of guys, but I just didn't have it in me to go through them. At this point, dating was starting to sour my stomach.

Garrett still hadn't reached out which meant the judge

had probably denied his bail. I couldn't imagine they had enough evidence to keep him unless they had found the money.

I texted Luke.

Did Garrett get out on Bail?

Almost instantly the little bubbles appeared indicating Luke was typing his reply.

No. Judge denied bail.

Why?

Because he's a murderer . . .

I clicked off the screen and tossed the phone onto my bed next to where Babbitt and Fizzy were snuggling as if they hadn't had a crazy morning.

Garrett didn't have multiple personalities. There had to be another explanation. Especially since I could see him in my future.

My heart leaped in my chest, a mixture of excitement and anxiety.

We had only been on two dates. And he was in jail. If there was going to be a future for us, I had to talk to him about what was going on. I had to ask him if he had multiple personalities.

I arrived at the jail an hour earlier than I had the day before. I didn't want the girl at the counter to have any reason to deny my visit. My plan was flawless, I would hold up a note to the glass, out of view of the cameras, asking if he had multiple personalities. I only hoped he would be honest.

"I'm here to visit Garrett Henry again." I smiled at the same girl who had helped me the day before.

"I'm sorry, I can't let you see him." She looked back at me with an icy stare.

"But why not? Did Luke—"

"Luke did nothing. Garrett doesn't want visitors."

I nearly choked on my own spit. "Visitors as in me? Or has he had other visitors?"

"I am not at liberty to discuss this with you. If you don't have anything else, I'm going to have to ask you to leave."

"But I need to talk to him. It's crucial."

She shook her head once. "I don't care how important it is, he doesn't want to see you."

"So it is just me then?"

"I didn't say that." She looked down at the papers on her desk. "He doesn't want visitors. Please leave."

I stood there for a moment longer.

"Rylie." Luke stood behind me, his hands on his hips. "I need you to come with me."

The girl behind the glass looked up and blushed.

"I was leaving. Geeze." I threw my hands in the air and cleared my throat trying to clear the tears clouding my vision.

"No, I need you to come with me," he said motioning at a door I hadn't been through before.

"Why?" I crossed my arms over my chest. "Am I under arrest now too? Do you think I'm a murderer too?"

Luke's face was turning red. "Don't be ridiculous."

"Then why?"

"Just please come with me."

"Fine," I said and followed him.

"It may be my fault he doesn't want to see you," Luke said as we walked down a corridor that had offices on both sides.

"What do you mean?"

"Well, we questioned him this morning after we listened to the recording of your conversation yesterday."

"Why? I didn't say anything."

"You mentioned something you knew about the boat," Luke said. "So we asked him. He probably wants to make sure you don't incriminate him any further."

Knife. Twisted. I was only trying to help. "I didn't mean anything by the boat."

We came to the end of the hallway and walked out a door leading to a huge parking lot surrounded by tall barbed-wire-topped fences.

"What's going on?" I asked Luke. "Why are you taking me to the impound lot?"

"We brought Garrett's boat and truck here to search more thoroughly—and we did."

"And did you find anything?" I asked trying to keep the emotion out of my voice.

"Enough to get Garrett's bail request denied."

They'd found the money after all.

"Okay," I said. "And . . ?"

"We found fibers in the cab of Garrett's truck matching the ones from the blanket that covered the first body you found."

Not the money, but definitely enough for the judge to think Garrett did it. Dammit.

"But now we're taking a closer look at the boat."

He led me around a row of cars that looked like they'd been there for months, to where Garrett's boat and truck sat side by side. Uniformed officers looked like an infestation of ants invading a yummy picnic basket. They were inside, underneath, and all around it looking for something they'd missed.

My heart pounded out of control. They were going to find the money and then Luke would know that I knew about it and then . . . what? Would I be arrested for impeding an investigation?

One officer stood on top of the seat where I had

slipped revealing the cash. One slip and he'd uncover the same thing I had, and then Garrett would be toast.

"This may be a good time to come clean." Luke looked down at me. "What were you talking about when you mentioned the boat?"

I was in a corner. "There was nothing. I don't know why I said that. I must have been talking about how I thought I saw two people in the boat, but I was obviously mistaken and—"

Luke held up his hand, and his face softened. "Cut the crap, Ry. I can only protect you if you're honest with me."

I shifted my weight from one foot to the other. Why did he think I needed protecting? "Okay." I took a deep breath. I had to fess up. "The other day I was—"

"Luke, we got something over here." One of the officers called out.

Shit. They found it.

Luke looked torn. "Hold that thought," he finally said. "I want to hear the rest of that sentence."

I began to follow him closer to the boat, but he stopped me. "Stay here."

Yeah, not likely. The moment he turned back to the boat, I tiptoed slowly behind him.

"Right here, it looks like this bench seat opens. But it's wedged shut." The officer showed his attempt to open the lid. I didn't know I'd closed it so securely, though the officer had been standing on it.

"Use the crowbar," Luke said, and one of the other officers handed up a crowbar.

"You can't destroy his property," I objected and every

head turned to look at me. I puffed up my chest and put my hands on my hips.

"I thought I told you to stay back there," Luke growled in my direction.

"You aren't the boss of me." I sounded like a sixteen-year-old arguing with her mother.

"Well? Open it," Luke barked at the officer holding the crowbar.

He looked from Luke to me and back again.

"She is not your boss, I am," Luke said. "Pry it open."

I could feel the gazes shift from me to the seat as the officer wedged the bar under the piece of wood and push down with all his might. The wood crackled under the pressure.

The entire group held a collective breath.

Finally, the top popped off, clattering to the metal hull of the boat.

We all leaned in to get a better look.

A disappointed sigh stole through everyone but me. Mine was in surprised relief.

It was empty.

Wait.

How was it empty? Where had all the money gone?

"Keep looking," Luke grumbled coming to stand at my side. "You were saying?"

"Was I? I've forgotten."

Luke quirked an eyebrow. "About the other day."

"Yeah, I don't recall." I couldn't tell him about the money. Not now. Not when it was gone and if I had told him before he might have been able to use the evidence to convict Garrett.

"I find that very hard to believe." He eyed me. "I know you think Garrett is innocent and you're trying to protect him, but there is a murderer on the loose and if Garrett is the murderer . . ."

"But he's not. I know he's not. Maybe someone is setting him up." Or maybe it's his other personality.

Luke nodded. "It's a possibility. But if that's the case, then the murderer is still out there, and if he or she thinks you're trying to find them, they'll have no problem killing you too."

"Then I need you to help me find the real killer."

"No. I'm not helping you. I will find the killer. It's my job. You're a park ranger—not that there's anything wrong with that," he added quickly, "but you're not an investigator. You don't even have a gun. And I don't think you know Garrett as well as you think you do."

"What do you mean?"

Luke looked down at his feet. "I don't know. But something doesn't seem right. I can't pinpoint it, and he's not talking at the direction of his lawyer, but this isn't the type of case you should be getting involved in."

"Does this lot have cameras?" I asked.

"Yeah." Luke looked confused. "Why?"

"Maybe you should take a look at them."

Someone had stolen the money from the boat, and it couldn't have been Garrett because he was still in jail. If they found the person who stole the money, they'd probably find the killer.

"Why won't you tell me what you know?" Luke asked reaching a hand out to touch my arm.

Part of me wanted to. But I was in too deep. At this

point, I would definitely be charged with stealing evidence, messing with a crime scene, and probably as an accessory to murder or something crazy like that. And if I was charged with those things I'd never get the full-time job. "Just look at the cameras. They might help clear Garrett's name."

Luke let out a sigh. "You're not going to stay out of this are you?"

"I'm going to try," I said.

"You really care about him, don't you?" he asked, his tone defeated.

"I guess I do," I replied as gently as possible.

He looked back over at the boat. "Come on, I'll walk you out."

I had an idea of where I could find more information, but first I had to stop by Garrett's house and pick up some more food for Babbitt.

When I pulled up to the house, a short raven-haired woman was making her way up Garrett's front steps. She stuck a key in the lock and opened the door, closing it behind her.

What the hell? Was this the girl that belonged to the lacy bra? Her boobs were big enough to fit the profile.

I marched up the steps and opened the door to find raven-hair standing in the kitchen.

"Hello," I shouted.

She pulled one earbud out of her ear. "Who are you?" Her nose stud and gauged earlobes added to her badass who cares attitude. And she made it look so good. Ugh.

"I could ask you the same thing." I crossed my arms over my chest.

"I'm here to clean the house, duh."

Duh? Did she just duh me? "You're a housekeeper?" Her tight jeans and black tank top weren't exactly what I imagined a housekeeper would wear. "Where are all your cleaning supplies?"

"In my car." The look on her face was a challenge to question her further. "Just because I don't look like someone who would clean houses doesn't mean I don't."

A housekeeper *would* explain the extreme tidiness of his home.

"Are you his dog walker or something?" Her narrowed eyes and the way she stood at the ready made me uneasy.

"I—I'm his—" Friend? Girlfriend? "We're—uh —dating."

"You're his girlfriend?" She looked me up and down. "I didn't know he had it in him. I mean, there was that one time, but otherwise, I assumed he was mostly gay." She shrugged.

Before I could ask what she meant about that one time, she continued. "Have you seen him lately? I haven't gotten my payment for the week, and my stash is getting low if you know what I mean." She held two fingers up to her mouth acting like she was taking a drag from a joint.

"You haven't heard?" I asked.

"Heard what?"

"Garrett's in jail for the murder of Boy Boy—you know —the drug dealer."

"Yeah, I know him," she said. "Saw in the paper he broke out of prison or something."

"And now he's dead."

"And they think Garrett killed him?"

"Don't you watch television? It's been all over the news."

"Television's for wankers." She touched her nose stud. "Can't trust anything anyone says on it."

"Well, he's in jail."

She furrowed her brow. "How long have you been dating?"

"Not long," I admitted. "But I'm on his side. I know he's a great guy. I'm working with the police to clear his name." She didn't need to know that I wasn't *officially* working with the police.

She stood there looking at me for a moment, her face still not giving away any emotion. "Then you should probably check out the secret basement and the rando that comes through here every once in a while. Might be related."

"What rando? What's a rando?" I asked but she was already at the front door. "Can you help me?"

"Uh, no." She turned the handle and walked out.

Rude.

I huffed over to the door I assumed led to the basement and shook the handle. Locked.

I slid my fingers over the top of the doorframe. No key. I rummaged through the drawers in the kitchen. Nothing.

I texted Shayla.

Do you know what a rando is?

She texted back in seconds.

you don't know what a rando is

> *No, that's why I'm asking you.*

it's what we call someone random. someone we don't know

By 'we' she meant people younger than me, people her age.

Thanks.

Not that that helped me in any form or fashion. I hadn't seen anyone but the cops and the housekeeper here. No randos to be found.

why

> *No reason.*

uh-huh ok......

I ignored her and shoved my phone back into my back pocket. I needed to get to the bottom of all of this.

M y knock was heavy on the solid wood door that probably cost more than my car. Like most places, Prairie City had its upper, middle, and lower economic classes—and the homeless, of course—but this area, the neighborhood surrounding Golden Rock Trail, was home to a higher-than-usual upper echelon of society. It was the ultra-ritzy where many of the wealthiest people in Colorado lived if they wanted to be a bit removed from the Denver metro area.

I knocked again, and a woman who looked to be in her mid-fifties opened the door a crack.

"Can I help you?" Her voice sounded like she'd just woken up even though it was mid-day and she had a full face of makeup and perfect wavy brown hair.

"My name's Rylie. I'm a park ran—"

"Yes, I know who you are."

"The snake video?"

She shook her head. "Tinder."

"But, uh—"

"Not for me, for my son. I swiped right, I haven't heard back from you. I didn't expect you to show up on my doorstep though."

"I'm not here about Tinder. I'm actually seeing someone." My mind was reeling. I tried to gather my thoughts. "Can I ask you a few questions about something that happened on the trail the other—"

"This again? The cops already asked me a bunch of questions. I didn't see anything." She tried to shut the door in my face, but I'd wedged my flip-flopped foot into the jam.

"Ouch," I said.

"Well, you shouldn't put your foot in people's doorways. Now get out of here." She looked around behind me as if she thought someone might attack in this ritzy neighborhood. "I don't need any extra attention coming my way. If you and your guy don't work out, check out my Elijah." She tried to shut the door again.

"I really need to know if you saw anything that might help," I pleaded. "The police have the wrong man. I need to find out who did this."

She opened the door a bit wider. "It's bad enough all of this crime ended up in my backyard. I don't need to be the next one missing a head."

"So you did see something?"

"Course I did."

I put my hands on my hips. "I'm not leaving until you tell me what you saw."

She looked scared as she searched the empty street

behind me. "Fine." She motioned for me to come inside. "Hurry up."

I took a step inside before she slammed the door behind me. I was greeted by a huge expanse framed by two staircases on either side of me, a gigantic picture window overlooking Golden Rock Trail, and a life-size autographed photo of Eli Hudson mounted on the living room wall. Apparently, everyone *was* a fan.

"I'm Marlene." She held out her hand in the daintiest of ways.

I shook it carefully. "Thank you for talking to me."

"I've kept this all bottled up for so long. It's probably best I talk to someone. Are you going to tell the police?"

"Do you want me to tell the police?" I asked.

"I guess it doesn't really matter. It's not as if I did anything wrong."

"That is true." I didn't really know if keeping information from the police was considered a crime, but it probably wasn't exactly moral.

"Come with me. Early every morning, before the sun comes up, I sit on my porch watching for wildlife. That day I watched as two thugs murdered that scrawny little man."

"Two thugs?" I asked. My insides clenched.

She nodded. "Both looked like they were big enough to be linebackers."

"Broncos fan?"

"My son plays for them," she said pointing at the photo of Hudson. "Otherwise, I wouldn't know what a linebacker was."

"I'm sorry, you're Eli Hudson's mother?" I stopped in

my tracks. Now that I knew it, I could see the resemblance. Mostly around the eyes.

"Of course. What woman would have a huge photo of a random football player framed in their living room?"

I could name a few.

"I actually met him a few days ago. Not that he'd remember. It was just at a signing. Does he know you've put him on Tinder?" And he was matched with me? My heart did a little flip-flop.

She looked at me, tapping her slippered foot on the hardwood floor.

"Sorry. You were saying?"

She nodded and continued out to the enormous deck suspended onto the back side of the house. "I was here"—she pointed to a chair—"and they were there"—she pointed to the trail where we had found the body.

"Wasn't it dark? How did you see anything?" I asked.

"Porch lights. Everyone leaves their back deck lights on at night. It lights the path up really well."

"Can you tell me exactly what happened? From the beginning?"

"It was quite odd. The one—Boy Boy, I'm assuming—carried the gun with one hand and pulling the scrawny man along with the other."

"And what was the other large man doing?"

"He followed along. I couldn't hear what he was saying, but it didn't seem to make Boy Boy very happy."

For not wanting to talk, this lady sure was doling out some serious information. "Go on."

"So they got to right there"—she pointed at the spot in the trail where we'd found the body—"and I knew something was going to go down. I grew up in the hood—the only little white girl on the block. I've seen my fair share of bad things."

My mind struggled to reconcile the image of this woman growing up in the hood and the woman sitting before me. The one who looked and spoke like she could be headmaster at a preparatory school.

"Is that when Boy Boy shot him?" I asked.

"Well, first they fought a bit. It looked like the big white guy was trying to stop Boy Boy, trying to talk reason into him. But then it looked like Boy Boy might shoot them both so the big guy got out of the way and Boy Boy shot the scrawny guy." She took a breath. "The white guy didn't watch him shoot the scrawny guy but had a blanket with him and covered the dead guy with it before following Boy Boy back from where they came."

"And where was that?"

She pointed to a row of trees behind which sat the parking lot where I'd first met Garrett little more than a week before.

"Did you call the police at this point?"

She turned and walked back into the house. "I thought about it. But right after he killed the scrawny guy, Boy Boy looked up, and I think he saw me watching. He pointed his gun in my direction as a warning, I'm sure because there's no way he would have hit me from such a long distance with such a tiny gun."

There was the hood talking.

"So I did what I did when I saw things go down in the hood. I minded my own business. The guy was dead. There was nothing I could do to save him. And if I'd tried,

I might have ended up with my own head missing like that girl they found at the other reservoir."

She likely didn't know that only a few minutes after she saw Boy Boy kill the boy, he had died himself.

"Thank you," I said. "I really appreciate you speaking with me." I wasn't sure if this exonerated Garrett, but it certainly made it sound like Garrett was in the right. If it was him there with Boy Boy in the first place.

"Can I get you a cup of tea or coffee?" she asked hustling to the kitchen. "I don't have company very often."

I hesitated. I really needed to speak to the Three Amigos before the sun got too high and the fish stopped biting, but the sadness in her eyes gave me pause. "Coffee, please. But just one cup."

Her face lit up. "Cream? Sugar?"

"Yes and double yes," I said. She poured us each huge mugs of steaming coffee from her fancy stainless steel coffee pot. "Thank you."

"So you said you met Eli? How was he? A gentleman, I hope?" She led me into the living room where oversized leather chairs looked like they hadn't been used —well—ever.

"I did. But like I said, he probably doesn't remember—"

"Of course I remember you," a booming voice from behind me nearly made me spill my coffee down the front of my white tank top. "How could I forget Prairie City's very own snake wrangler?"

He plopped a kiss on his mom's cheek, and she beamed up at him. As for me, it was all I could do not to let my jaw hang open. He was even more handsome out of uniform. His sleek physique and wavy brown hair, just like his mom's, looked photoshopped even though he was standing right in front of me.

"I'm sorry I scared you." His laugh was almost silent— a whisper. But it made his green eyes squint a tiny bit at the edges.

"How did you get in? I have a security system."

"You're going to have to change the code from my birthday if you want to keep me out." He poured himself a cup of coffee and came back to sit on the couch across from us. "Is Dad away on business again?"

Marlene nodded. "I keep trying to get him to retire, but he's worried we'll fall back on hard times."

"I'd never let that happen," Eli said. "I'll talk to him. He shouldn't be leaving you alone, especially with all the crime around here. Maybe we should look at getting you a different house. Somewhere safer. Like Cherry Creek?"

"I have enough firepower in this house to protect the entire population of Prairie City. Not that they need it now that that criminal is dead."

She sure talked a big game in front of her son. When I'd first arrived, she looked like a scared old woman.

"Okay, Mom." Eli held his hands up in surrender. "I just don't want anything to happen to you."

"Thank you, darling." Her smile was the same one I got from my mother when I told her I'd ironed my laundry. Pure love and pride.

"We're being rude." Eli turned to me. "Rylie, was it?"

He remembered my name?

"Yes."

"What brings you to my mother's house?"

A fake Nikki giggle escaped my lips and was instantly disgusted with myself. "Sorry. Um, I was just here—"

"She wanted to ask about the murder I saw." Marlene took another sip of her coffee.

"You saw a murder?" Eli's eyes widened as he looked from his mother to me and back again.

"Yep." She put the mug down on a stained glass tile coaster. "If you came around more often, I'd be able to tell you these things."

"Have you spoken to the police about it?" He asked his mother then turned to me. "You're not a cop, right? You're a park warden or something."

"Park ranger, and no, she hasn't spoken with the police."

"We have to speak to the police immediately." He pulled his mom up to a stand. "We're going down to the station to tell them everything."

Great. So Luke would know Garrett was for sure with Boy Boy. Heck, he'd probably even get Marlene to identify him.

"I know the police. I work with them a lot. I could pass along the information." I hated lying, but I wanted—needed—more time to figure out what was going on.

Marlene patted her son on the hand. "Rylie's a good one. She has it under control. Plus, I don't want to go down to any gross police station."

Eli seemed torn. He probably knew the right thing to do was to take her down, but for some reason, he looked like he wanted to trust me.

I stood and walked towards the door. "Thank you so

much for the coffee, Mrs. Hudson. And thank you for speaking to me. I hope it will help get an innocent man out of jail."

"That man I saw on the TV?" Marlene asked.

"Yes. I don't think he really killed Boy Boy," I said.

"Oh, well I'm sorry to tell you this, but I'm sure he did," she said.

"What? Why?" I asked.

Eli stood off to the side taking all of this information in.

"Because he was most definitely the man who was with Boy Boy that day. And when Boy Boy shot that scrawny guy, that other man looked murderous." She frowned. "I'm guessing he did it not too long after I saw Boy Boy fire that gun."

No. She couldn't be sure it was Garrett. From her deck and in the dark, it was impossible to make out the details of someone's face.

"Didn't I see you with him at the meet and greet?" Eli asked, the puzzle pieces seemingly coming together in his mind. "He's an assistant or something right?"

"Accountant," I replied. "And yes. I was with him. We were—are—dating."

It looked like Eli's shoulders dropped a bit, but maybe *I* was starting to see things.

"Oh, honey. You don't want to date murderers. Even the ones that get rid of other murderers. They're still pretty bad." Marlene patted me on the shoulder.

I shook my head. There's no way he could have killed anyone. Even another murderer.

"Love is blind." She followed me to the door. "Would

you please come back again for coffee? We can watch for thugs off my deck." She whispered the last part in my ear so Eli couldn't hear.

"That would be lovely. Thank you, Mrs. Hudson."

"Marlene. You have to call me Marlene now. We're friends."

Eli Hudson's mom was my friend. This could easily be the weirdest day I'd ever lived.

"Okay, Marlene. Thank you. I'll see you again soon." She waved as I walked back to Cherry Anne.

The sun was high in the sky making the changing leaves on the Aspens glisten. The three amigos would definitely be leaving their fishing spots soon. I revved the engine and put it in gear before I heard a tap on my window.

Eli's face stared into my car. I hit the roll down button and put the car back in park. "What's up?" I asked.

"Eww, what's that smell?" he said taking a step back.

"What smell?" I asked sniffing the air like Fizzy always did. "I can't smell anything."

"Maybe it's out here," he sniffed, made a face, and then shrugged. "You're not going to tell the police what my mother told you are you?" Even up close his skin was so smooth, I'd think it had been retouched.

"Why would you think I'm not?"

"Because you obviously care way too much about this Garrett guy everyone's been talking about. And my mother's statements could probably secure his time in jail, couldn't it?"

I didn't answer. I wasn't going to tell him outright I

had no intention of telling the police what Marlene had said.

"Fine. Don't tell me. I'll just take my mom down to the station—"

"Can you give me a few days? Then you can take her down. If Garrett is the killer, he's in jail anyway. It's not like a few days will do any harm."

Eli thought about this for a minute. "I'll give you two days," he said. "Then I'm taking her down to the station."

Two days wasn't much, but it was all I had. "Deal."

"And thank you, by the way, for hanging out with my mom. She's been really lonely lately."

"Maybe you should hang out with her more often," I said, still a bit irritated that he was trying to oust Garrett as the murderer.

"I would, but I can't. With practice and all of these games, I barely have time to shower and eat."

"Well, it was my pleasure. You have a wonderful mother." I put the car back into gear. "Now if I may? I have to go find a killer."

"Maybe you should let the police—"

The rest of his sentence was drowned out by Cherry Anne's engine and the squeal of her tires as I drove away.

21

The Three Amigos were packing up their fishing gear when I pulled into the parking lot of Golden Rock Pond. It was practically empty minus a few trailers and pickup trucks.

I waved as I parked next to their old pickups with Vietnam Veteran license plates.

"Hey guys," I said stepping out of the car.

"Sweet ride, young lady," the black guy with white hair, a white mustache, and an eyepatch said.

"Thank you. We've never met before, but I'm Rylie Cooper. I'm one of the summer park rangers for Prairie City."

"You're the girl in the video with the snake, right?" the one with a limp said. "I saw it on the YouTube."

"The one and only." I smiled. At least he hadn't called me the snake wrangler.

"I'm Luther," the guy with the eyepatch said. "And these guys are Ray and Tom."

"It's a pleasure to meet the three of you." From what I could surmise, Ray was the tallest in a worn leather jacket and Tom was the one with a limp. Both of their white mustaches quirked up into big smiles.

"What can we do for you?" Tom asked.

"I don't know if anyone has spoken to you yet, but I wanted to ask if you saw anything out of the ordinary about a week ago. One of the other rangers and I were patrolling around the time we think Boy Boy Johnson was killed."

"Well it's about damn time someone asked what we knew," Ray said. "Them idiots don't even realize they have good informants right under their noses."

Luther let out a laugh. "Don't mind Ray. He's had a bad day of fishing, that's all."

"I had a better day than you, you old pirate."

Tom shook his head at the other two. They were like the sweet old grandpa versions of the Three Stooges. "We saw Boy Boy that morning with the man they have in jail if that's what you're asking."

"Just the two of them?" I asked. Maybe they'd seen them with the guy Boy Boy had murdered.

"Yep just the two," Tom continued as the other two looked on. "They were launching that tiny little boat, sipping their coffee."

"We didn't know it was Boy Boy until after they found him dead," Luther said in his deep crackly voice. "We thought he was some tired clown-looking guy."

"Tired? Why do you say tired?" I asked.

"He kept stumbling. Couldn't keep his eyes open but a fraction," Ray said. "The other guy was wide awake though. We can relate. Sometimes when we get out here that early, it's hard to keep our own eyes open."

He hadn't been tired. He had been drugged.

"And did you see them actually get into the boat together?" I asked.

"Sure did. It was a tight fit with all that crap they were carrying," Ray said.

"What kind of crap?"

"Oh fishing tackle and the like," Tom said.

"Plus that black bag."

The one with the head. I shivered.

"You all right?" Luther asked.

"I'm good," I said. "Thanks."

"And then we didn't really watch them much since we were setting up for the day. It wasn't until we saw the rangers—probably you and your partner—talking to them that we realized the one wasn't there anymore," Ray said.

"We assumed he was in the truck sleeping off whatever night he'd had before," Tom said, his tanned face turning white. "We never thought he'd have drowned in front of our very eyes."

I knew the feeling.

"It was kinda like that one time in Nam when the three of us were hiding from Charlie in that lake, and we all had reeds to breathe from," Ray said.

"And mine filled with water and I nearly drowned," Tom said. "I'm just glad you boys saved me so I could get back to see my wife and kids."

"It wasn't even an option. We couldn't leave without you. Not when we'd have to face Celia's wrath," Luther said with a nudge to Tom's arm.

"Anyway, that's what we saw," Tom said.

"What about the guy we talked to on the ramp. Did you notice anything about him when we were done speaking with him?"

"Just that he tore out of here really fast. His boat almost came off the trailer when he made the turn," Ray said. "We should have known then something was going on."

"Thank you for your help. And for your service."

They all stared at me with big eyes.

"What?" I asked.

"We don't often get thanked for our service," Tom said. "Vietnam was a war no one wanted. People have said some pretty cruel things to us over the years."

"Well, that's not who I am. My dad served too before I was born."

Luther smiled a big smile. Ray nodded. And Tom wiped a tear from the corner of his eye.

"Feel free to come back and ask us questions any time. We'll keep our eyes peeled," Luther said.

"Thanks again, guys." I got back into Cherry Anne and drove away trying to hold in my emotions.

It made me furious when people disrespected our veterans, and those guys were just as amazing as my own father. I'd be sure to pay them more visits in the future.

But for now, I had to decide if I'd go to Luke and tell him what I knew about Garrett. Every single thing I'd found had implicated him in the murder of Boy Boy. But maybe if I told Luke everything, he'd get less time because of self-defense or something.

22

Wednesday morning came and went and I still couldn't decide whether to tell Luke what I knew. By the time I'd gotten ready for work, I only had a few minutes at the local deli before I had to report to the reservoir for my shift. The lady behind the counter handed me my sweetened iced tea and turkey and cheese sandwich when I thought I caught a glimpse of something—someone—familiar out of the corner of my eye.

My stomach dropped. Garrett sat across the street on the patio of another restaurant. Why hadn't he called me when he was released?

I marched out the door unsure if I wanted to throw my arms around his neck or chew him out. The street between the restaurant and the deli was busy and loud, so when I called out to Garrett, it was no surprise he couldn't hear me.

As the traffic cleared and I was walking across the

street, Garrett stood and looked at the door to the restaurant, a smile spreading across his face at the sight of good old raven-hair.

She sauntered over to him, and he bent down so she could reach her arms around his neck. He lifted her off her feet and kissed her so passionately I nearly dropped my sandwich.

To my left, a horn blared and I realized I was standing in the middle of the street. I stumbled backward and ran to my car, hoping Garrett hadn't seen me. The minute Cherry Anne's door closed, I burst into tears.

How could he? I mean, I know I'd only met him on Tinder, but to so blatantly betray me? And with the housekeeper? Didn't he know I was doing everything I could to get him out of the murder charges? I'd spent my whole morning chasing down information when he'd been out of jail gallivanting around with another woman?

Right after my shift, I would take Babbitt back and then I would never see either of them again.

———

"What's up with you?" Antonio asked when I arrived for our closing shift.

"Nothing." I didn't want to talk about seeing that lying, cheating, no good sneak of a man. And here I thought he was still in jail.

"It doesn't look like nothing," he said looking at where I'd slammed Cherry Anne's car door after pulling out my duty bag.

"I'm just an idiot." I threw the bag into the summie truck. "And my car stinks."

"Smells like mine does when I don't put baking soda in my boots. And I don't think you're an idiot."

"When it comes to judging men, I am." I plopped down in the truck and closed the door while Antonio stood outside the window. He motioned for me to roll it down, even though the truck windows were automatic. I obliged. "Let's get this shift over with, shall we?"

"Do you know what helps me think when I'm stressed out?" He asked, his tough-guy façade melting away ever-so-slightly.

"What?"

"Driving the boat."

"Well, we both know that's not going to happen," I said.

"Come on. I'll take you out. Maybe I can show you some skills Ben couldn't." Typically he would have said this in a way that sounded dirty, but today he seemed genuine.

That was probably why I agreed and found myself at the helm of the dreaded ranger boat yet again.

"I don't think I ever thanked you for standing up for me to Ursula," I said as I pushed the throttle forward making the boat jump from the slip.

"Whoa. Easy there." Antonio covered my hand with his own and pulled the throttle back a bit. "Be gentle on the beast. She has feelings."

I tried to keep my mind on the water, but with him so close it was hard.

"And I didn't really stand up for you. I merely told

186

Ursula what she would be missing if she got rid of you. Ursula and upper management are driven by numbers. All I had to do was inform her that you're bringing in lots of paying guests."

"Well, thank you." I turned the bow towards the open reservoir. Thankfully, there weren't many park visitors to witness me sinking the boat.

"Now I want you to look at the water around you and feel the boat's movements." Antonio moved back to the other side of the boat, leaving me to control it myself.

I tried to remember the steps Greg had taught us. The things Ben had mentioned.

"No. Nope," Antonio laid a hand on my shoulder. "Get out of your head. Breathe and look around."

I sucked in a breath and let it out. The water was pristinely calm, the changing aspen trees motionless on the shoreline.

"That's better. Now head over to those buoys, and we'll do some practice."

"How do you want—"

"Stop. Stop thinking so much. Concentrate on the sounds the boat is making, the feel of the engine when you move the throttle, the beat of the water as it hits the hull."

I tried to concentrate on the things he'd mentioned. The boat purred like a kitten with a ball of string. The engine's vibrations resonated through my boots when I pushed the throttle forward. The water lapped up on the bow forming a beautiful tail of curved wake behind us.

"Very good." Antonio closed his eyes almost as if he were praying.

"I'm sorry about Kyle and your wife."

His eyes blinked open, and he looked at me like I was a ghost.

"Why in the world would you be sorry about either of those two?"

I turned the wheel a bit towards the buoys, the boat reacting well to my actions. "It's just that I know this summer's been kinda rough on you with losing your best friend and your wife and I feel partially responsible."

"Oh Rylie," Antonio said, "You are most definitely not responsible for any of that. It has been a tough summer. But it's not your fault. Kyle was a murderer. I vouched for him, and he nearly killed you. And my wife, well, let's say, it's been over for a long time. This was just the last straw. Neither of us was happy."

"But you don't seem happy without her either," I pushed.

Antonio looked down at his boots. "For the past ten years, I've known exactly what my life would look like. That all changed overnight. I'm not unhappy because I no longer have my wife."

"Did she end up leaving you high and dry like you thought she would?" I asked.

"You remember our first fight?" Antonio smirked. "She actually didn't. Couldn't. The judge ordered everything be split 50-50."

"That's good. I'm glad it worked out as well as it could have."

"Rylie, do you realize you've been expertly maneuvering the boat for the past five minutes?"

I looked out at the water in front of us. The buoys

were to my right. I had done one of the drills Greg taught us on the first day without so much as a hiccup.

"I did it," I squealed.

"Don't get too excited. You still have control over this boat," Antonio said, but the smile on his face beamed with what I thought might be pride.

"Now you don't feel like an idiot, do you?"

Irritation swelled in my belly when the thought of Garrett and raven-hair came rushing back. "Thanks for reminding me."

"Sorry. But the boat helps, right?"

"I guess so." It did help me forget. "Let's go back in the coves and see if anyone's catching anything."

Antonio nodded. "You know, it's not your fault men are idiots. And it doesn't make you an idiot for trusting the wrong men."

"It does make me an idiot for consistently going for the cheaters though."

"Maybe you have a type," Antonio said.

I turned the wheel and the boat effortlessly carved through the water back into Muddy Water Cove. "Garrett and my ex, Troy, were about as opposite as you could get."

"From what I hear, Garrett was a bit of a tool on the boat ramp when you met him."

These guys were worse with gossip than women. "I guess so. But other than that—and today—he was probably one of the nicest guys I'd ever dated."

"Multiple personalities?"

"Carmen." I shook my head.

"What?" Antonio held up his hands and shrugged.

"Who don't you talk to?" I asked.

"Basically, nobody. Everyone loves me." The cocky Antonio peeked through but was quickly replaced again with the one who seemed to be more caring. "I'm a good listener if you ever need to talk."

"I'll keep that in mind." I scanned the shoreline of the cove, but there weren't any fishermen. "You and Nikki are close too, right?"

Antonio shifted his weight from one foot to another. "We are friends."

"Do you know why she hates me so much?" I asked.

"You're not exactly nice to her," Antonio replied.

"I'm not the bad guy here. She started in on me the minute we met."

"And you didn't help the situation."

I reflected on my behavior. I may not have been super warm to Nikki, but I hadn't been an outright jerk like she had either.

"One of you will have to make the first move in a positive direction. And I'm thinking it's not going to be Nikki."

"I don't understand though. She's the one who got the full-time position. She's the one everyone loves. And she's the one who's dating Luke." The last part slipped out before I could stop it.

Antonio tried to keep his face neutral at my outburst. "If this is about a guy, I don't want to hear about it. Nikki talks enough about Luke. It's all Luke this and Luke that. Luke isn't paying enough attention. Luke stares at other women. Luke is just dating me to make Rylie jealous."

"Wait. What?" I pulled the throttle back into neutral,

and the nose of the boat dipped towards the water sending Antonio into the console in front of him.

"I shouldn't have said that last part." He steadied himself back on his feet.

"Is that what she really thinks?"

"That's what she says everyone thinks. His co-workers, his partner, even her parents."

"That's beyond ridiculous. Luke's not the type to use someone."

"He probably isn't doing it intentionally, Rylie. Men usually don't. But deep down, if that's what he's doing—and I'm not saying it is, but if it is—he knows."

I yanked the throttle in the backward direction because we were drifting into the shore and watched as the backside of the boat pushed through the water, its struggle mirroring the one going through my head. It was as if I were trying to herd a million thoughts and feelings with a snow shovel.

"Look. I probably shouldn't be telling you this, but Nikki is threatened by you. Jealous even."

I scoffed. "What does she have to be jealous of?"

Antonio shook his head and rubbed the back of his neck. "You really don't give yourself enough credit, you know?"

"Nikki is practically a model. A rich model. Everyone here loves her. She's good at everything she does. There's really no comparison."

I pointed the boat back to the dock across the lake and slammed the throttle down. Even if Antonio wanted to say something, I wouldn't be able to hear it in the wind.

Did Luke really still want something with me? Was I

really even considering something with Luke when I hadn't yet officially ended things with Garrett? And what about Antonio? His manly façade had dissolved on the water. There was something endearing and almost sexy about that. He hadn't once tried to hit on me, hadn't once said or done anything suggestive. Why are men so damned confusing?

"Uh, Rylie?" Antonio said to my left.

"What?" I snapped back.

"You just—"

He pointed, and I expected to see something I'd run over, but instead, I found that I'd managed to back the boat into the dock like I'd seen the other rangers do so many times before.

"I did it," I practically screamed.

I jumped up and down as Antonio secured the boat with ropes to the dock. When he came to a stand, he smiled down at me. "You did it. See that wasn't too hard was it?"

I fought the urge to throw my arms around his neck. "Thank you for helping me get out of my head."

"Any time," Antonio said.

23

B abbitt sat in the passenger seat of my car as I called Luke. After staying up all night replaying Garrett kissing raven-hair, I finally decided I had to tell Luke what I knew. The phone rang five times before his voicemail picked up.

"Luke, it's Rylie. I have so much I need to tell you. It's about Garrett. He's not innocent. I thought he was but he's not. I have statements from witnesses. Please call me."

I pushed the end button and looked over at Babbitt. "I hope you like raven-hair because your daddy is going to jail for a long time."

Babbitt let out a low yowl. I patted his head, feeling sorry for the sweet ball of fluff. Everything had been so perfect. Garrett and me, Babbitt and Fizzy. How stupid was I? How many guys had to cheat on me before I found one who wouldn't?

When I pulled up to Garrett's house for the last time,

yet another woman stood at his door. But this one didn't seem to have a key as she was knocking. Her legs were as long as a super model's, and her hair was a beautiful shade of honey brown.

"He's not here," I said stepping out of the car.

The woman turned, and Babbitt bounded up to her.

"Hello Babbitt," she said, her voice older than her face let on. "And Rylie, I presume?"

"Yes." I held out my hand confused.

"I'm Babbitt's grandma, Helen," she said, affectionately scratching Babbitt behind the ears. "Garrett's told me so much about you."

Did he tell her about raven-hair too?

"It's nice to meet you," I said. "I was dropping Babbitt off. I don't think Garrett and I are going to be seeing each other anymore."

"It's all this police business isn't it?" she asked. "He's innocent, you know?"

"I thought so too, but I don't think I know him like I thought I did."

"Garrett's a good man, the best of all my boys by far. In fact, he's always taking care of the others. There's no way he killed anyone. He's never even had a speeding ticket."

I wondered if she knew her son might have multiple personalities and probably *had* killed Boy Boy? I decided I wasn't the person to break the news to her.

"Oh, I'm glad you're here. I have a gift for you, from Garrett." I had completely forgotten the box in my trunk. I let Babbitt into the house before she followed me down to my car.

"That's so sweet of him to have my gift already," she

doted. I did my best not to roll my eyes. Why wasn't he here greeting his mother instead of with one of his many girlfriends?

I clicked the button on my key fob, and the trunk popped open.

"What is that smell?" she asked immediately recoiling and covering her nose with her hand.

I inhaled deeply and instantly regretted it. The smell of something rotting made my insides heave. Had I left my leftover lunch in my work bag?

"I'm sorry, it's probably my old lunch containers." I pulled the box from the trunk and handed it to her, slamming the lid down before more of the smell could escape.

"I think the smell is coming from this box," she said doing her best not to gag.

She was right. The smell hadn't dissipated at all.

"Maybe you should open it," I said. Garrett hadn't mentioned it needed to be kept cool or anything.

She peeled back the tape and lifted a black duffle bag from inside the box.

Before I could stop her, she unzipped the bag. It only took two seconds before she vomited all over what I knew she saw.

It was the bag missing from Garrett's boat. The bag Boy Boy had been carrying with hair sticking out on the trail cams. The bag containing the dead woman's head.

24

"We have to turn this over to the police," I said, zipping the bag back up without looking inside.

"My son, Garrett. H-he's—" She wretched again.

I pulled my phone out of my pocket again and dialed Luke's number. Again, it went to voicemail. "Luke, seriously. Call me. I have evidence you need to see."

I popped the trunk again and put the bag and the box back inside. Just the thought of driving around with a severed head in my trunk made me sick.

"Helen, we should probably go inside and wait for the police," I started but before I could take a step in her direction a silver car with black tinted windows came barreling down the road at us.

"Helen?" I reached out for her hand as she was still crouched on the ground heaving.

The car was not slowing but picking up speed.

"Helen," I yelled and yanked her by the arm out of the way just as the car flew past us. "Get in the car. Now."

I don't know if it was my tone of voice or nearly being run over, but she listened. I fired up Cherry Anne, tearing away before the car could make a u-turn and come back at us. I turned down a side street away and gunned the accelerator.

"Is someone trying to kill me?" Helen finally said, her perfectly makeuped face streaked with trails of tears and vomit.

"I don't think you, per se." I didn't want to consider they were trying to kill me. Why wasn't Luke calling me back? I glanced at my phone screen. No notifications. I took a right towards the police station.

"Do you think we got away?" Helen asked.

I looked in my rearview mirror as the silver car turned onto the road behind me. From the driver side, a handgun emerged and fired off two shots taking my side mirror. Dammit, that would cost a pretty penny to replace.

"Not yet." I mashed on the accelerator as Helen let out a squeal. If my cheater ex had taught me anything, it was how to drive like a cop.

Cherry Anne bolted like her wild mustang namesakes.

Helen held on as I turned down street after street, her face a nasty shade of green.

"What if we give them the head? Maybe then they'd leave us alone."

"We've seen too much, Helen. The only way we're getting out of this is to make it to the police station." Even if Luke wasn't there, someone would be, and they'd know how to get in touch with him.

But after several turns, I was utterly lost. Every time I thought I'd gotten rid of the silver car, there it was. It was like they had a GPS tracker on me.

Somehow we managed to make it back to Garrett's house where Garrett stood out front. He waved as we approached, a big smile on his face.

I glanced in the rearview mirror, the silver car was gone, at least momentarily.

"Open the garage," I shouted out the window at Garrett. His face was confused, but he did as I asked, running inside and opening the door. It was tormentingly slow as it opened and I inched Cherry Anne inside.

Once inside, Garrett pushed the garage door button, and it slowly began to close.

"What's going on?" he asked.

"Someone is trying to kill us," Helen said throwing her arms around his neck. "They have guns."

"Let's go inside and you can tell me everything," Garrett said.

I hesitated. If Garrett was the killer, I needed to get away as quickly as possible. But it was either him or the people in the silver car. I ran my hand over the phone in my back pocket. If Luke wasn't going to respond, I'd have to call the police. That's probably what I should have done in the first place anyway.

"Rylie, are you okay?" Garrett asked. Helen turned to look at us.

"Fine," I said, not wanting to make a scene in front of his mom. "Let's go inside."

He bent down and kissed me on the cheek. "Everything is going to be okay. I'll take care of it."

I walked past him into the house. There was no way I was going to rely on him to get me out of this situation.

25

Babbitt greeted us when we entered. He gave Helen and me a big slobbery kiss but stopped short of Garrett. His hackles raised and he let out a low growl like he had at the dog park before he'd chased the person in the hoodie away.

"What's wrong Babbitt?" I asked looking from him to Garrett who had a panicked expression on his face.

"I must smell like the jail," Garrett said. "It's okay buddy."

Babbitt continued to growl but let Garrett past him to the door leading to the illusive secret basement. "You can hide down here until the police come," he said motioning for Helen and me to go downstairs.

Helen smiled and started down the carpeted stairs, Babbitt following closely behind.

"I need to use the restroom. I'll be right down," I said.

Garrett hesitated. "Okay, but hurry."

I nodded and went to the bathroom in the hallway—

the same one I'd been in the first time I'd been in his home. It was amazing how quickly things had changed. Thoughts of the severed head in my trunk made my insides squirm. What was I doing here? I needed to leave.

I flushed the toilet to mask my voice as I called 9-1-1.

"9-1-1 what's your emergency?" the dispatcher asked.

"I need assistance." I gave her the address and hung up the phone. I probably should have stayed on the line, but I couldn't risk Garrett hearing me. I smoothed down the front of my shirt and opened the door running straight into Garrett's chest.

"Who were you talking to?" Garrett's face was twisted into a mean grin.

"No one. I—"

"Cut the bullshit, Rylie." He grabbed my arm and pulled me to the doorway to the basement. "Get down there."

I held my ground. "No. I need to leave."

"You leave when I say you can."

"Is this your other personality? I need to speak with Garrett, please."

Garrett let out a loud laugh. "Get. In. The. Basement."

He looked like he was ready to push me down the stairs, so I turned and walked down myself, hearing the door lock into place behind me. I only hoped the police would get there in time.

The basement was a makeshift bedroom set up in the finished living space. An unmade bed was pushed against one wall and trash littered the floor. It was too bad the housekeeper, or whoever she was, didn't clean down here too.

I sat on a leather recliner as Helen folded clothes off the floor. Babbitt nudged my elbow with his snout, and I scratched him behind the ears. "What's going on buddy?" I whispered.

"I thought you were dating Garrett," Helen finally said.

"I *am* dating Garrett," I replied surprised by her sudden comment.

"So then why was Derrick kissing you on your cheek?" she asked without looking at me.

"Is Derrick the name of his other personality?"

"Whose other personality?" She turned to look at me, a frown on her face.

"Garrett's. I know about his—er—disorder."

It took her a second to reply, but instead of recognition, she burst out laughing. I was absolutely tired of people laughing at me.

"What?" I asked. But she couldn't catch her breath. She was hysterical, probably because we had nearly died.

"Helen, why are you laughing?"

She finally stopped long enough to say, "They're twins. Identical."

My heart felt like it stopped. Twins? There were two of them?

"They've always done this with girls. But it's usually Garrett covering for Derrick when Derrick couldn't decide between two girls. This time Derrick hooked you for Garrett."

"What do you mean, Derrick hooked me?"

"He's the one you met the first time at the pond."

Derrick. Not Garrett. Had Garrett told Luke he had a twin? That that twin was likely the murderer?

I grabbed my phone and dialed Luke's number. The call wouldn't go through. No service.

"So upstairs that was—"

"Derrick, of course. It's a shame you can't tell them apart. Even Babbitt can."

"I didn't know I had to tell them apart."

How had I not known I was practically dating two men?

I told Babbitt to stay and walked back up to the top of the stairs. The door was still locked. I tried to pull on the handle, but the double-sided deadbolt held the door in place.

Faint voices that sounded like Derrick and a woman— raven-hair—were arguing. I pressed my ear against the door.

"She's my mother, you can't kill her," Derrick yelled.

"You let Boy Boy kill my sister, what's the difference?" she said.

"I didn't *let* him. Boy Boy did whatever he wanted. I didn't know he was going to kill her until it was too late."

"He gave you her head." The woman's voice cracked with emotion. "And you gave it to that bimbo park ranger." Bimbo? Ouch.

"I thought it'd be our lifeline, you know?" Derrick pleaded. "Like we could frame her for the murder or something."

"She's in with the cops, you idiot. And you should leave the scheming to me. The only thing you got right was getting rid of Boy Boy."

"He killed my best friend right in front of me," Derrick

203

said in a low growly voice. "He deserved to die for what he did to me. To you. To all of us."

"Don't get fresh." The woman's voice was indignant. "You've screwed everything up. And now I have to fix it."

"Just leave my mother out of it, please."

"She knows too much, Derrick. And so does that stupid park ranger," the woman said. "This was supposed to be easy. We would get the money, take out Boy Boy, and move on with life."

"We can still do that," Derrick said. "My mom will keep her mouth shut. Your sister's head is in Rylie's car, and I know you can figure out a way to pin the murder on her."

I sucked in a breath. What a douche.

"Where's the money?" She asked.

"It's . . . safe."

There was a pause.

"No." The woman sounded like she was about to murder Derrick. "You didn't leave it down there."

Did she mean in the basement?

"I can't believe you," her voice grew louder as she approached the door. "Now, I have to kill them."

"I'll go down there and get the money. We'll leave them there. The cops will find them eventually. By then we'll be long gone." Derrick's voice was pleading.

"We're not running away. This is my turf, my city," she said, and the sound of a gun slide loading a round into the chamber set my feet in motion.

"Where would you hide something down here?" I asked Helen.

Helen looked up from making the bed. "What do you mean?"

I scanned the room. "If you were Derrick, where would you hide something? Something important?"

"He always used to hide candy in the heat vents. One time he forgot and it got cold and the whole house smelled like burnt chocolate."

My gaze came to rest on a heat vent in the ceiling above the bed. I jumped on top as Helen let out an angry groan. "I just made the bed."

"Helen, your son and the woman who I assume was chasing us in the silver car are about to come down those stairs." I yanked on the metal grate. "The head in the back of my car shows you exactly what they are capable of." A small lie, since Boy Boy was the one who had killed the girl. "The woman wants us dead, and I'm not sure Derrick can prevent it."

Helen was wide-eyed listening to my every word.

"When they come down, they're going to be looking for money." I yanked one more time, and the grate popped open. A plastic bag filled with bundles of cash tumbled to the bed. "This money." I picked it up and replaced the metal grate, shoving it back into the ceiling.

"What are you going to do with it?" Helen asked.

"I don't know yet," I said.

At that moment the door popped open. Helen's gaze shifted from me to our impending doom. While she was distracted, I shoved the bag of money under the bed kicking it as far back as possible with the toe of my Adidas.

"Get back against the wall, both of you," raven-hair

said coming into view down the stairs. She had the pistol pointed at our heads.

Helen let out a squeak. I grabbed her hand and pulled her over to the wall.

"We're not going to hurt you," Derrick said.

"He may not hurt you, but I make no promises. Get the money," raven-hair said to Derrick.

He jumped on the bed making Helen cringe next to me, her perfect bed-making skills literally trampled on twice over. The grate popped out of the ceiling more easily than he had expected and he came tumbling down to the floor with the grate in hand.

"Get up, you idiot," raven-hair said. "Get me my money."

Derrick climbed back onto the bed and glanced over at me. I raised an eyebrow. I know he didn't want his mom to die, but I was of no consequence to him.

"It's not here," he said under his breath. "It was just here." His entire forearm was up the vent searching for the bag.

"They did something with it," raven-hair said.

"We most certainly did not," Helen said, her voice more confident than I could have produced. "I am very disappointed in you, Derrick."

Derrick looked from raven-hair to his mother. "I-I'm sorry, Mom."

"You and your brother need to quit jerking women around. This poor sweet girl doesn't deserve it."

"We didn't mean it." He looked at me apologetically. "At least Garrett didn't. I saw Rylie and set them up. That was supposed to be the extent of it. You know how hard it is for Garrett to talk to women. He didn't even know I saw Rylie after that. He thought I had left town."

"Wait," I said. "When exactly did you pretend to be Garrett?"

"Just that night at the park when I gave you the—er— gift for my mom." He looked back at Helen. "Sorry, I didn't mean for you to ever actually get that."

Raven-hair cleared her throat. "Enough with the family counseling session. Where. Is. My. Money?"

"I don't know," Derrick said.

"I do," I said.

Raven-hair turned the gun barrel at me, and I immediately regretted my admission.

Where were the police? They should have been here by now.

"Are you going to tell me where it is, or am I going to have to shoot you? Don't worry, I won't kill you right away." She aimed the gun at my legs.

"I'll tell you if you let Helen go." I needed the distraction, a way to get the gun away from raven-hair.

"I'll let her go if you tell me where my money is."

Derrick looked back and forth between us.

"I don't understand why you think it's your money. Did you earn it?" I was stalling, and it would likely get my leg shot off, but at least it would give the cops time to get here and arrest these two.

The thought of my mother's face flashed before my eyes. I couldn't let her find me in a hospital bed again.

"Sure, I earned it."

"Legally?" I asked.

"You're not a cop, you're a park ranger," she said stepping closer to me.

Babbitt growled from where I had ordered him to stay.

"You were the one at the dog park, weren't you?"

"Wow, it took you long enough to figure that out."

"Why were you there?" I asked.

"I saw you and Derrick together at the reservoir the night he gave you the head. I saw you kiss."

A smirk washed over Derrick's face. Their mother should be proud, both boys knew their way around a kiss.

"I thought he was Garrett."

"I should have done away with you then and there. It would have made all this business so much easier."

She had been there to kill me? I looked over at Babbitt who seemed only ready to rip her head off at my command. But I couldn't risk him getting shot.

"So you and Derrick are an item?" I asked.

"Were."

"Noted," I smirked in Derrick's direction.

"Don't get any ideas." Her voice quirked up a bit. "Dead people can't date and you most certainly will be dead before today is over."

"I don't want to date him. I've got a thing for his brother."

"The rando nerd." She rolled her eyes. "Why? He's a bore."

"He's nice. You should try a nice guy for a change. Well, once you're out of prison, that is. I'm assuming that money came from drugs—that you're part of Boy Boy's gang."

"Me? Part of his gang? Ha!" her nostrils flared, her

nose ring sparkling in the lights. "Boy Boy was the face of *my* gang."

"I'm impressed," I said. Helen squeezed my hand beside me and my gaze shot to the stairs where the tip of a gun was coming around the corner. I could only hope it was the police.

When raven-hair's head began to turn to follow my gaze, I shouted, "The money is under the bed."

She stopped and glared at me. "Get it." Her gun was pointed at my face now.

I walked over to the bed and bent down feeling several eyes on my backside. Babbitt's growls were barely audible.

My head was still under the bed when I heard Luke's voice from the stairs. "Freeze. Put the gun down."

I quickly pulled myself up to see raven-hair turn her gun on Luke.

"Babbitt sick," I said. And Babbitt was on top of her in seconds, his teeth circling the back of her neck.

Derrick turned and tried to run past Luke, but Luke pulled him to the ground with one arm. Jerry moved more quickly than I had ever seen to cuff raven-hair.

"Can you call off the dog?" he hollered.

"Babbitt, come," I said, and Babbitt came to sit next to me. "Good boy." His tail wagged at the sound of my praises.

"It's about time you showed up," I said to Luke.

"We've been outside but had to figure out how to get in without anyone getting hurt." He reached up to the mic on his chest and said, "All clear inside."

Helen was on her knees now, her face scrunched up

with tears streaking down her cheeks. I crouched in front of her. "Are you okay? You were brilliant."

"Thank you. Thank you so much," she said wrapping her arms around my neck. "You were amazing. I thought she was going to shoot you."

"So did I," I replied.

At that moment I felt another set of arms around me. I turned to look and Garrett—the real Garrett—was crouching behind me with tears in his eyes. "I'm so sorry. I should have told you."

"It's okay, we can talk about it later," I hugged him back. It was going to take some time to reconcile the fact that he had a twin brother and that I hadn't been able to tell them apart.

"So about that head . . ." Luke said.

26

Raven-hair and Derrick were both charged with various crimes. It was unlikely either of them would be out of an orange jumpsuit anytime soon.

"I'm just glad you didn't end up in the hospital this time," Shayla said after I finished telling her the story.

"Me too. I can't imagine my mother's reaction if I had." Thankfully, they'd managed to keep my name out of the news about breaking the case.

"Are you still going to date Garrett?" We were both applying makeup in the mirror in the loft exercise area. We each had our interviews—mine for the full-time ranger and hers for police academy—and had just finished working out to combat some of our jitters.

"I think so. I mean, it's not his fault all of this happened. Plus he was pretty amazing when I take out the parts that were Derrick."

"That has to be confusing," she said.

"It's getting easier." Garrett and I had spent hours every night for the past week talking about everything and even more hours making out before I forced myself to go home and sleep. "I'm even taking him to meet my parents tonight after the interview."

"Wow. So Luke—"

"Is dating Nikki and we're just friends." I pushed away the conversation I'd had with Antonio. I couldn't live life waiting for Luke to come around. "What about you and Seamus? Are you going to come out as a couple soon?"

"Probably at the season end party tonight," she said. "He's really fun to be with but do you think it's weird he's so much older than I am?"

"Nah. If the two of you make each other happy, that's what matters."

She smiled. "It's time."

We both took one last look in the mirror and headed off to our respective interviews.

When I walked into the banquet hall, I expected to see Ursula and the other higher-ups that had interviewed me the last time. Instead, Ursula sat in the middle of all of the full-time rangers.

"Is this my interview?" I asked feeling like I'd walked in on a meeting I wasn't supposed to be in.

"It is. Sit down." Ursula gestured to a chair in front of them. All of the rangers had a smile on their faces except for Nikki who had her arms crossed over her chest. "Thank you for coming today."

"It's my pleasure," I said knitting my hands together in my lap so I wouldn't pick at my cuticles.

"At the suggestion of my boss, your peers are going to be making the decision whether or not to hire you. I will simply be overseeing the process."

Hopefully, she hadn't been the one to come up with the questions.

"We'll go by rank. Each ranger will ask one question and any follow-up questions necessary to clarify."

I nodded and looked at Greg who smiled in a way that would calm any nerves.

"Rylie"—he looked down at the notecard in front of him—"you have been with us for a season and have done very well. Can you tell me why you would like to be a permanent member of our team?"

This was an easy one. "This job has been the most enjoyable one I have ever had. The rangers are professional and fun and truly love what they do. I would be lucky to join such a team and do something I enjoy day in and day out."

"Thank you," he said and looked at Antonio.

"Hello, Rylie." Antonio quirked up one side of his mouth.

"Hi." I smiled back.

"If you were to be hired as a full-time ranger, would you feel as though it was too boring if there wasn't a murder every single day?"

I knew he was joking, but I couldn't answer the question more emphatically. "Absolutely not. In fact, I'd be happy to never see a dead body again."

Everyone besides Nikki and Ursula laughed along

with me.

Ben continued. "Rylie, your boating skills need work."

My chest constricted. I didn't know how to tell him I'd actually improved drastically. "Yes, they do," I said, and Antonio shot me a frustrated look.

"What will you do to make sure you are properly skilled to use the boat for the remainder of this season and seasons to come?"

"I plan on doing additional training with whichever ranger is scheduled with me now that the season is winding down. If I need to spend hours out on the boat every day, I will do that to make sure I can use the boat if needed."

Antonio waggled his eyebrows as if I was saying he and I would spend hours on the boat together. I ignored him as best I could.

"Thank you, Rylie," Ben smiled as if he were proud of my answer.

"Seamus?" Ursula said.

Seamus nodded. "Do you promise to never talk to me before my first cup of coffee is gone if we're ever scheduled to a morning shift together?"

The other rangers snickered. Ursula looked like she might come out of her seat and strangle him.

I put my hand over my heart. "I do so solemnly promise."

"Good." He winked at me. "Dusty?"

Dusty, whom I had never worked with, looked at me and then down at his notecard. "Well, you and I have never actually worked together, but I want to give you a hypothetical question."

"Okay," I said.

"If you were walking along a trail doing a foot patrol and came across a homeless camp where several people were standing around an open flame, what would you do?"

This one was tough. I didn't know much about homeless camps or how to handle them other than what Seamus had told me.

"First, I'd have them put out the fire since we are under a burn ban."

Dusty nodded and took down a note.

"Then I would give them a warning about moving their items and give them locations of the nearest homeless shelters."

"And if you came back two days later and they still hadn't packed up?" Dusty asked.

"At that point, I would ticket them and confiscate their property." I think that's what I was supposed to say.

"What if they didn't want you to take their items?"

Seriously? How was I supposed to know?

"I'd probably call for backup from either another ranger—you or Seamus since you know most of them—or the police."

"Thank you," Dusty said nodding.

"But I'd still urge them to find refuge in a shelter," I added before they could move on. "I wouldn't want to leave anyone on the streets, but I know it's not legal to set up homeless camps within the city."

Dusty smiled, and Seamus gave me a thumbs up.

It was Nikki's turn.

"I would like to know why you don't like me," Nikki said, and every eye turned her way.

Ursula looked as if she might say something, but stopped herself and then looked at me with an evil smile on her face.

"I-I don't not like you," I said. It was a lie, but how could I tell the truth?

"You don't like me. Everyone knows you don't. I want to know why before I am to choose whether or not I want to work with you indefinitely."

The tension in the room was as thick as the fog that descended over the reservoir in the early mornings.

I took a breath. Honesty was always the way to go. "Okay, you're right, I don't like you. And I know you don't like me, but you're not the one being asked why."

She smirked and tilted her head.

"From day one you hated me because I broke some stupid training record. I guess it was just a bad first impression."

"That's not true. You don't like me because you love Luke and I'm dating him. It's jealousy, just say it."

Her outburst took everyone aback. All eyes were wide.

"I'm dating someone else, Nikki. Luke and I are in the past. And that has nothing to do with our working relationship."

All of the men looked down at the table in front of them.

"I would, however," I continued, "like to ask you for your help if I am hired on as a full-time ranger."

"Help with what?" she spat.

"Help with the boat. You're exceptionally good at

maneuvering it, and I have a lot to learn." Kill her with kindness as my mother would say. "If you had some extra time, I'd love for you to teach me what you know." Especially since I wasn't a complete and total loser at driving the boat now.

Nikki let out a grunt. "We'll see."

"If that's all?" Ursula interrupted. All the heads bobbed minus Nikki's, which was now looking down at her hands. "We'll let you know what we decide."

I took that as my opportunity to leave. "Thank you for your consideration," I said before walking out of the room.

27

Garrett showed up on my parents' doorstep promptly at 6:00 that evening. We were going to have supper with them and then head out to the bar for the season-end party.

"You look beautiful," Garrett said holding a massive bouquet of summer flowers.

I had on a floral maxi skirt and a pink tank with a jean jacket over top. Fall had finally settled in and required more clothing in the evenings.

"These are for your mother," he said.

"Oh they're beautiful, thank you," Mom said from behind us. "Come in, come in."

She ushered him into the dining room where my entire family sat their eyes wide. It had to be especially difficult for them to differentiate him from Derrick who was plastered on the television every night for the murder of Boy Boy.

"This is Garrett Henry," I said and introduced him to everyone.

"It's a pleasure to meet you. Your daughter is an absolute joy." He squeezed my hand, and we took our seats at the table.

"I'm sorry to hear about your brother," Tom, Megan's husband, said.

"Thank you." Garrett smiled. "But he's getting what he deserves. I love him—he's my twin—but after all his lies, I can't bring myself to protect him anymore."

The night after Derrick was taken into custody we'd talked for hours. He explained why he hadn't just told me about his brother—that he was afraid at first that I'd fall for Derrick over him since Derrick was more charismatic. Then he thought Derrick had skipped town and didn't want to let on that he knew about Derrick's involvement with Boy Boy's gang. He and the police—Luke especially —had been working closely to catch Derrick.

"Rylie tells us you like the Broncos," Dad said. "You know it's our favorite team."

"I do. Rylie has recently enlightened me on the intricacies of football. I see many games in our future. I could probably even swing tickets for all of you to join us at a game."

This was met with various thank-yous and words of excitement. All of the earlier tension about Derrick melted away.

"You were amazing with my family," I said as we pulled into the bar where we were having the season-end party.

"Your family is amazing. You're lucky to have them."

"I truly am." My insides warmed. "How's Helen doing?"

"She's back in Florida. All the excitement here was a bit overwhelming and she had to retreat to her quiet place."

"I hope to see her again. She was flawless under pressure. You should have seen her boldface lie to that killer lady."

"She had to deal with my brothers and me growing up. She's always been pretty tough."

"Speaking of your brothers, how is Derrick?" I asked. We hadn't talked about the subject much because I hadn't wanted to pour salt into a wound.

"He's doing okay. Even though I know it's right that he's behind bars, I still have a hard time with the fact that I couldn't help him."

This was not completely true. Garrett was paying his big-name attorney to defend his brother in hopes he'd get a reduced conviction due to his taking down a notorious gang member.

I squeezed his arm. "You're a good brother, you know that?"

He smiled and gave me a quick kiss. "Thank you."

We walked into the bar hand-in-hand, and Shayla waved. Seamus had his arm proudly around her neck, and she was downright beaming.

"I got in!" she said as I approached.

"Oh my goodness, that's amazing." I hugged her tight.

The reservoir wouldn't be the same without her, but we'd stay in touch.

"So did I," Brock said.

"Wow, congratulations," I said trying to hide my lack of enthusiasm.

"And we're expecting a baby," Brock said rubbing Bella's completely flat stomach.

"Brock, you weren't supposed to tell anyone yet," Bella said. "We're only six weeks along."

"Sorry sweetie, I'm just so excited," Brock was glowing more than Shayla and Bella put together. I couldn't help but smile for him.

The other rangers, minus Nikki, sat around watching and sipping their beer.

Garrett pulled out a stool for me and helped me sit before taking the seat next to me. Several of the guys' eyebrows raised, but they said nothing. They could take notes on how to treat a lady. Antonio looked awkwardly away, trying not to make eye contact.

"Oh, now that Nikki's here, we have some news too," Greg said.

Nikki and Luke walked towards us not holding hands but with smiles on their faces. Maybe Luke wasn't dating Nikki to make me jealous after all.

My heart raced, but I didn't know whether it was seeing them together or the news that Greg was about to spill.

"We'd like to introduce our newest full-time ranger," Greg said tapping his beer glass with a fork. "Rylie Cooper."

Shayla and I both let out squeals. Garrett wrapped me

up in his arms and planted a huge kiss on me before Shayla pulled me away and into an embrace of her own.

"Thank you so much," I finally said to the rangers. "I won't let you down."

"I just can't believe we hired the shit-magnet, snake wrangler." Seamus's joke was met by laughter. Even Nikki smiled.

Now all I had to do was find a place to live that wasn't my parents' basement.

THANK YOU FOR READING
SUCKERED

I would be honored and eternally grateful if you would post a review on Amazon and/or Goodreads about the book.

Also, I love hearing from readers! Email me at stellabixbyauthor@gmail.com and sign up for my newsletter at www.stellabixby.com for exclusive content and up to date information about upcoming books in the Rylie Cooper Mystery Series.

XOXO,

Stella

ACKNOWLEDGMENTS

It's my favorite part of the book . . . thanking the people who helped me along the way!

God must come first. Thank You for giving me strength, perseverance, and a love for writing.

Nolan, thank you for believing in me. I couldn't do this without you. I love you.

Faith, thank you for being a teenager I like to be around! I love our nightly chats and our one-on-one time.

Lily, this one's for you, kiddo! Thank you for helping me pick out the release date and the book cover! I love you so much!

Grant, thank you for FINALLY taking naps in your crib. You are such a light in my life.

Dad, thank you for being one of the first people to read SUCKERED.

Mom, thank you for reading both books and helping me with edits!

Keri, I can't wait to hear what you think of this one!

Lurea/Mom, thank you for beta reading for me and for loving my books so much. I can't wait for you to read book 3!

And to the rest of my family, thank you. I appreciate all of the love and support you freely give!

Jenny, another amazing cover! Your talent is amazing! Thank you!

Shawna & Matthew, thank you for reading SUCKERED and getting your comments back to me so quickly! I can't wait to send you book 3!

Joel, thank you for your help with the title! Even though I know this isn't exactly your genre . . . ha!

And again last but not even close to least, thank you to every single person who reads this book. I hope you enjoyed reading it as much as I did writing it!

ABOUT THE AUTHOR

Stella Bixby is a native Coloradan who loves to snowboard, pluck at the guitar, and play board games with her family. She was once a volunteer firefighter and a park ranger, but now spends most of her time making up stories and trying to figure out what to cook for dinner.

Connect with Stella on Facebook, Twitter, and Instagram @StellaBixby.

Stella loves to hear from her readers!
www.stellabixby.com

CPSIA information can be obtained
at www.ICGtesting.com
Printed in the USA
LVHW022225210221
679522LV00005B/331

9 780999 602126